Brian Aldiss was born [...] Second World War he se[...] East. He began his prof[...] career as a bookseller in Oxford and then went on to become Literary Editor of the *Oxford Mail*. For many years Brian Aldiss was a film reviewer and poet. The three outspoken and bestselling novels making up *The Horatio Stubbs Saga* (*The Hand-Reared Boy* (1970), *A Soldier Erect* (1971), and *A Rude Awakening* (1978)) brought his name to the attention of the general book-buying public, but in the science fiction world his reputation as an imaginative and innovative writer had long been established. *Non-Stop*, his first SF novel, was published in 1958, and among his many other books in this genre are *Hothouse* (published in 1962 and winner of the Hugo Award for the year's best novel), *The Dark Light Years* (1964), *Greybeard* (1964) and *Report on Probability A* (1968). In 1965, the title story of *The Saliva Tree*, written as a celebration of the centenary of H. G. Wells, won a Nebula Award. In 1968, Aldiss was voted the United Kingdom's most popular SF writer by the British Science Fiction Association. And in 1970, he was voted 'World's Best Contemporary Science Fiction Author'. Brian Aldiss has also edited a number of anthologies, a picture book on science fiction illustration (*Science Fiction Art* (1975)) and has written a history of science fiction, *Billion Year Spree* (1973). The three volumes of the epic Helliconia trilogy, published to critical acclaim, are *Helliconia Spring* (1982), *Helliconia Summer* (1983) and *Helliconia Winter* (1985).

By the same author

Fiction
The Brightfount Diaries
The Primal Urge
The Male Response
The Hand-Reared Boy
A Soldier Erect
A Rude Awakening
The Malacia Tapestry

Science Fiction
Non-Stop
Galaxies Like Grains of Sand
Equator
Hothouse
The Dark Light Years
Greybeard
Earthworks
The Saliva Tree
Cryptozoic
Barefoot in the Head
The Eighty-Minute Hour:
   A Space Opera
Enemies of the System
Report on Probability A
Frankenstein Unbound
Moreau's Other Island

The Helliconia Trilogy
Helliconia Spring
Helliconia Summer
Helliconia Winter

Stories
Space, Time and Nathaniel
Starswarm
The Best SF Stories of Brian
   Aldiss
Intangibles Inc., and
   Other Stories

The Moment of Eclipse
Seasons in Flight
Cosmic Inferno
Last Orders
New Arrivals, Old Encounters

Non-fiction
Cities and Stones
The Shape of Further Things
Billion Year Spree
Hell's Cartographers
   (with Harry Harrison)
Science Fiction Art (Editor)
This World and Nearer Ones

Anthologies and Series
   (as Editor)
Best Fantasy Stories
Introducing Science Fiction
The Penguin Science Fiction
   Omnibus
Space Opera
Space Odysseys
Evil Earths
Galactic Empires 1 & 2
Perilous Planets

With Harry Harrison
Nebula Award Stories 2
Farewell Fantastic Venus!
The Year's Best Science Fiction
   (annually from 1968)
The Astounding-Analog
   Reader (2 volumes)
Decade 1940s
Decade 1950s
Decade 1960s
The SFs Masters Series

BRIAN ALDISS

Brothers of the Head
and
Where the Lines Converge

PANTHER
Granada Publishing

Panther Books
Granada Publishing Ltd
8 Grafton Street, London W1X 3LA

Published by Panther Books 1979
Reprinted 1985

Brothers of the Head first published in Great Britain by
Pierrot Publishing Ltd 1977
Copyright © Brian W. Aldiss 1977
Where the Lines Converge first published in *Galileo*
magazine 1977
Copyright © Brian W. Aldiss 1977

ISBN 0-586-04994-0

Printed and bound in Great Britain by
Collins, Glasgow

Set in Intertype Times

for darling WENDY
first to hear of
The Bang-Bang
rockin-anna-rollin
in the back of a Volvo
proceeding
like a bat out of Hell
from Hunstanton
'Well, I was shocked . . .'

Contents

Introduction   7

Chapter 1
Henry Couling's narrative   11

Chapter 2
Laura Ashworth's report   31

Chapter 3
Excerpt from taped interview with Nickolas Sidney   50

Chapter 4
Zak Bedderwick's narrative   53

Chapter 5
Continuation by Roberta Howe   61

Chapter 6
Statement by Dr Alyson Collins   75

Chapter 7
Conclusion by Roberta Howe   81

Appendix   103

WHERE THE LINES CONVERGE   109

Introduction by Roberta Howe

This volume is a memorial to the unhappy life of my brothers – their strange, unrealized, dual life. Although it ended in murder, and many people who like to pronounce on such things have said that my brothers' entire existence was a form of slow murder, they did enjoy happier times. It is not an easy matter for any of us to weigh up the balance of joy and sadness in another life, even one as close as my brothers' was to mine. Perhaps when we grow up we should not be so concerned with judging such things, but simply get on with the job.

When Tom and Barry were young lads, they did not realize that they were marked out from all other children. One thing was as strange to them as another, all was accepted without questioning. Father took us to live on L'Estrange Head when mother died, at which age I was only a tot of three and the boys mere babies. In the wild surroundings of the Head, we children were thoroughly at home. We all loved this beautiful spot in which I still remain. I'm thankful they returned to the Head in the end, before the last act of their tragedy was played out.

We could name all the plants growing on the Head, thanks to the teaching of our father. Down in the salt marshes, where the land is still regularly washed by the tides, grows a plant called the grass wrack. The wrack is often immersed in the sea for long periods. It can even flower under the water, and nature so provides for it that its pollen is water-borne. I often think of that humble plant in connection with my dead brothers. They also had their flowering, however submerged it might have been.

Nobody can deny that our family, the Howes, and the

neighbours on the mainland, with few exceptions, looked on poor Tom and Barry as a stigma, a freak of nature. The boys, poor innocent mites, were never properly forgiven because mother – who was greatly liked by everyone – died in giving birth to them. At the height of the boys' fame, when they were universally popular, the feelings against them changed to feelings of pride. But there was never any real concern for their terrible situation and, when the end came, back came the old disgrace. Ever since, I have known ostracism, useless to deny it.

Laura Ashworth, who played a positive part in the life of Tom and Barry, would perhaps say that the only shame lay in feeling shame, in these enlightened days. But it must be remembered that we live in a remote and backward part of the country, and that the Howes had their origins here. Little has changed on the coast of which L'Estrange Head forms part. Indeed, there has been recession rather than progress, for my Aunt Hetty has told me how Deepdale Staithe was a fine harbour in her young day, until the channel silted up. It would be impossible for a grain boat to navigate now.

Of course, with my brothers' lives always beside me, as it were, I am still torn with emotion when I let myself dwell on it. I was unable to write their story myself, not only because of strong feelings but through my incapacity as an author; so I have put together what has been said by others concerned in the drama.

Going through the pages that result, I can only reflect that Tom could have become a happy man but for the last twist of ill fate. Most of his life was still before him. As for Barry – there was so much more to him than the anger and violence on which many people have dwelt. Barry hated his fate even more than Tom; yet hatred was not the only feature of his nature, by any means.

As for 'the other' . . . I'm long over my horror now, and think of it as one more grain ship that never sailed. 'The other's' channel to the sea was silted up even before it came into being. Pity seems to be more appropriate than fear or shame.

Here I wish to thank all who contributed to the narrative, with particular thanks to Laura Ashworth for her counsel and to Mr Henry Couling for financial aid. I thank Paul Day for permission to publish excerpts from his songs.

I also have to thank John James Loomis of the Canadian Broadcasting Authority for permission to include part of a taped interview made in connection with his TV biography, 'Bang-Bang You're Deadly'.

CHAPTER 1

Henry Couling's Narrative

I am a partner in Beauchamp-Fielding Associates, a London firm of solicitors who have built up a particularly valuable connection with what is commonly called 'the pop world', which is to say the legal and managerial problems connected with the exploitation of cheap music and young people. My first encounter with the Howe twins, Barry and Tom, came as a result of this aforesaid valuable connection. I was acting on behalf of Bedderwick Walker Entertainments.

Since the Howe twins represented a somewhat special case, I had agreed to see them, and more particularly their father and legal guardian, in person. I took an Inter-City train from King's Cross to Lynn, where a car awaited me to take me to Deepdale Staithe, a hamlet on the North Norfolk coast. It is a desolate part of the country. Civilization has scarcely obtained a foothold there, in all the centuries these islands have been occupied. No doubt a permanently active east wind has much to do with this state of affairs; only a moron would hesitate before fleeing to the nearest city.

The bleakest point along this stretch of coast is arguably L'Estrange Head, a natural feature lying between the summer resorts of Hunstanton and Sheringham. It is neither a true headland nor a true island. To determine its geographical status under law, one would have to decide whether its baffling system of marshes, creaks and rivulets link it with or divide it from the mainland.

There was not at that time, and I imagine there is still not, any way whereby one could drive a car on to L'Estrange Head. The lanes which strike out towards the marshes from the Deepdale Staithe–Deepdale Norton road, to wind across Deepdale Marsh and Overy Marshes, peter out in bog, or at

11

embankments built long ago to guard against the floods which perpetually harass this unfortunate coastline. One can imagine that the entrenched attitudes of the locals is such that their initiative may run to dykes but never to roadways.

Be that as it may, one chilly April day I found myself stuck in Deepdale Staithe for half-an-hour, while my chauffeur persuaded a local man called Stebbings to take me by boat out to the Head, where the Howe family had its residence.

Stebbings was what might be termed a character. He was a young man, still in his teens, not unprepossessing, with a sandy sprout of beard and a habit of not quite looking you in the eye. He handled his boat and its snorting engine nonchalantly. Throughout the whole trip, he insisted on talking to me in the local dialect. I scarcely listened, so busy was I huddling in my coat and endeavouring to keep warm. The wind came in chill off the North Sea.

We took a winding channel which, according to Stebbings, was called 'The Run'. The tide was low and we progressed between mud banks for the first part of the way. So we got into the harbour and then through more open stretches of water. The view all round was desolate in the extreme. I could make out a couple of ruinous windmills standing above the expanses of reed and grass, then my eyes watered, and I resigned myself to wait. The motion of the boat made me queasy.

At last, Stebbings – who had obliged me by naming every sort of bird which flew over – brought us to the Head, to a beach which he called Cockle Bight. A short plank walk served as a jetty. He helped me ashore.

'I hear you be a-going to buy they twins off of old Howe,' he said.

'I suppose half of Deepdale Staithe knows my business, since there can be nothing else to talk about here.'

'A rotten bit of business it is, if you ask me.'

'I was not asking you, Mr Stebbings, thank you all the same.'

He said nothing to that, looking away from me. I asked him the way to the Howes' house and he pointed to a low blob in the distance. A slight apprehension passed over me; I made him renew his promise to return for me in two hours, before the incoming tide could prove too formidable an obstacle for his engine. He then swung his boat about and headed back to the Staithe with a cheery wave to me. I was left standing on my own.

The Head was a solitary place, built of shingle and sand, sparsely covered by vegetation, open to whatever weather the heavens chose to deliver. It was hard to imagine why anyone should wish to live here – but imagining was not my trade. Business brought me here; business would take me away again.

Cockle Bight was an extensive half-moon bay of sand which gave place to low grey dunes. I looked at the pebbles and stones beneath my feet. Every one of them carried, on their westward side, a tiny fan of sand, where a few grains had found protection from the prevailing wind. That same wind whined about my ears. On all sides were water and low land, the two elements divided by strips of sand or reed. The reed was always in motion. Deepdale Staithe was just visible across land and water. Stebbings' boat had already disappeared round a bend in the channel. To one side and ahead lay open water, the unwelcoming North Sea. I took one look at this wilderness and set off towards Howe's place, holding my coat lapels about my throat.

Hundreds of tern wheeled up from a concealed lagoon, sped seawards, and disappeared. L'Estrange is a bird sanctuary, preserved by the National Trust. Albert Howe is its warden. I could find no blot on his record of service. His is a job for those who prefer a lonely life, or have reason to wish to shun other people.

Terns and gulls were the only signs of life. Then I climbed

13

a line of dunes and saw two boys fighting some way off. Locked together, they stood in waving grass, their figures outlined against the waters of Deepdale Bay. They punched each other with concentration.

I paused. Isolation lent a supernatural quality to their violence. As I went forward again, the dark figures tumbled over and disappeared into a sea of grass.

Arriving on this bleak Head, one perceives only a flat and tumbled expanse of land, encroached on in most directions by the North Sea. However, a walk across it provides a different picture. I was following a faint track which led up and down through shallow depressions and low mounds; all about was a world of miniature valleys, narrow eminences, tiny cliffs, and secret hollows. Dunes of yellow and grey sand, scantily covered in vegetation, marched towards the skyline. These features had been shaped more by the forces of wind and water than by the passive ground itself, as bone is shaped by pressure of tendon and blood.

In order to negotiate a dale, I had to jump a clayey creek and climb a bank. There were the lads, fighting in a hollow almost beneath my feet.

I had heard no sound from them. The constant noise of air, water, and reed accounted for that.

Startled, I looked down at where they sprawled, fighting each other steadily with a machine-like hatred.

They might have been sixteen years of age. They were of similar build, stocky, with broad backs. They dressed similarly. They wore the nondescript blue jeans which were the prevailing fashion with young people of both sexes at that time, and woollen sweaters. Despite the chill of the day, they went barefoot.

The great difference between them lay in their faces. The boy who rolled with his back on the ground had fairish hair and a long face. His face was red with exertion; one eye had

14

been partly closed by a blow, so that he appeared to leer up at me with what would be termed in court 'a malevolent expression'. His cheeks were stained by tears and dust, his hair was full of sand.

His brother had black hair which stood stiffly up from his skull. His face was round, even squat, his brows low, his mouth bright and flat against his cheeks. He also glared at me. I saw immediately that this dark boy had a deformity, a second head, growing from his left shoulder.

These were the Howe twins, Tom and Barry.

'Hello,' I said. 'I've come to collect you.'

They turned identical surly looks at me, nimbly leaping up. I thought for a moment they were going to attack as they faced me defiantly. Then they turned as one, still locked together, and went bounding off across the dunes.

It was clear to see then that they were one, inseparably joined in the middle, just as my client had stated.

I stood watching them go, clutching my throat, rattled by coming on them so suddenly. They were making for the huddle of low buildings Stebbings had indicated as their home, the best part of a kilometre distant.

There was nothing to do but follow after, keeping to the trail which now led through rabbit-clipped turf.

Nearing the buildings, I came to a piece of ground which someone had at some time attempted to bring in to cultivation. A few cabbage stumps formed the sum total of its crop. More poor tokens of rural living followed: an old broken boat lying upside down, abandoned lobster pots, a collapsed workshed, a fenced patch of ground which contained a flower-bed and some hens in a coop. Beyond stood the house and another building.

The house was built of stuccoed brick up to window level and lath and plaster above that. One side was painted with tar or bitumen and was propped by a large old beam. The general impression was ramshackle.

Afternoon sun made the windows bleary. It was a sick-looking house. Paint had long since peeled from porch, door and window-frames.

An oddity of the site was that the house had been built directly to the south of a stone ruin, so that all view of the sea was excluded from its chief windows. Presumably the builder had intended to protect the house from the more savage storms blowing in off the sea. Ordnance Survey maps label the ruin L'Estrange Abbey.

Almost as soon as I had tapped on the door of the house, it opened and a man's head appeared.

'Yes.'

I said, 'I am Henry Couling of Beauchamp-Fielding Associates. You are expecting me.'

'You'd better come in.' Neither his face nor his voice betrayed much more expression than his window-panes. He never gave me his name, but it was apparent from the start that he was Albert Howe. Howe was in his early fifties, a spare man with a suggestion of strength about him. His complexion was brown and weathered, and brown was the colour of his sparse hair. His dress was a khaki shirt with a flapping leather jacket over it, stained cavalry twill trousers, and a pair of boots of vaguely military design. He stood aside to let me in.

It was not exactly a welcome, but I was glad to escape from the wind. The door opened straight into a parlour in which a fire of driftwood was burning. So cheering a sight was it that I immediately moved across to the hearth and stooped to warm my hands.

'Is it always as cold as this on L'Estrange Head?' I asked looking up at him. He remained – rather stupidly, I thought – by the door.

' 'Tisn't so bad today,' he said. 'We heard the cuckoo this morning, across them marshes.'

He jerked his head in indication of the direction of the marshes to which he referred.

16

His was a melancholy room. The ruin of the abbey cast permanent shadows into it. A light bulb burned overhead, picking out in sickly detail a profusion of birds and small animals which covered the walls. Rough shelving housed these stuffed mementoes of the living world outside; wherever one looked, dead eyes glinted. A well-loaded bookcase stood in one corner. Table and chairs and two old battered armchairs completed the furnishing. The room lacked, as they say, a woman's touch; despite the fire, it felt cold and damp, and smelt of old seaweed, as if high tide had been known to lap over the threshold of the door – a not unlikely assumption, I reflected.

A kitchen led off on one side, its door standing half-way open. A dog barked sporadically there, as if tied up and not hopeful of improving its position. I looked in that direction, to find two pairs of eyes observing me; two heads were immediately withdrawn.

As I rose, I saw that a loaf of bread and the leavings of a poor meal lay on the table, together with a dead seabird. The seabird was stretched out on a board with its pinions taped outspread and its gizzard slit open.

Howe came awkwardly back from the door and sat at the table, where he proceeded to finish a mess of bread, cheese and pickle on his plate. As if aware of a certain social boorishness in what he was doing, he glanced up at me and gave a jerk of his head, coupled with a quick funny expression and a wink, as if to say, 'This is the way I am.'

Drawing myself up, I said, 'I take it that you are Mr Albert Howe, sole surviving parent of the twins, Thomas and Barry Howe.'

'Tom and Barry, that's right. The twins. I expect you'd like a cup of tea. Robbie! Tea, gel!'

This last call was echoed by activity in the kitchen, and presently a girl came forth with a big brown teapot. Setting it down on the table, she poured a mug of tea and shyly proffered it to me.

17

She was a good-looking girl in a countrified way, with big hazel eyes and a complexion as brown as her father's. Her hair was plentiful, hanging down between her shoulder-blades in an old-fashioned plait or pigtail. Like her brothers, she wore faded jeans and went barefoot, a slovenly habit, especially in women. Her figure was well-developed; I judged her to be twenty years of age.

There was less unfriendliness in her gaze than in her father's. As I accepted the mug of tea and sat down, un-bidden, at the table beside the impaled bird, she said, 'So you are the lawyer as has come to take my brothers away.'

I patted the briefcase I had brought with me. 'I am acting on behalf of Bedderwick Walker Entertainments, with whom I understand your father is keen to come to an agreement. I have a copy of the contract here, Mr Howe, and will be happy to familiarize you with its contents. We can go over it clause by clause, if you so desire, provided I am able to meet Stebbings and his boat at your jetty in approximately two hours' time.'

Howe crammed the last of his crust into his mouth, masti-cated for a while, and then said, 'It's for the best, Robbie, I keep a-telling you. The boys can't hang around here for ever and a day, not now's they're growed up.'

'That's correct,' I said, snapping open the briefcase. 'The contract guarantees you and your sons a substantial salary, payable monthly, for a period of three years. It gives Bed-derwick Walker the option of renewal of contract for a further two years, at a fee subject to negotiation. Bearing in mind that Bedderwick Walker will invest a considerable amount of money in training and projecting your sons, the arrangements are eminently generous.'

'You're still taking my brothers away from home,' said the girl. 'Who will look after them, I'd like to know.'

Ignoring her, I spread the contract out before Howe, pushing aside the butter and a jar of pickle.

18

'I trust that your sons are ready to return to London with me?'

'They're willing enough to go, yes.'

He looked up with a helpless expression, and said to his daughter, 'Robbie, see as they're all packed, will you?'

As Howe picked up the contract to study it, I saw his hand was shaking. He had well-shaped hands, with long fingers. He watched Robbie as, without another word, she padded into the kitchen on her bare feet.

'It's hard to know what's best, Mr . . .' he said gazing at the dead bird as if addressing it. 'May and I got on so well, we helped each other with everything as came up. That's her in the photo over there.'

He pointed to a framed photograph of his dead wife, standing on the mantelpiece. A sepia face stared out at the world from under a large hat.

'I'm sure she would be happy with the contract as it stands.'

Still he wouldn't bring his attention back to the document.

'That May was a very fine woman,' he said. 'One of the best, that she was.'

I offered no comment.

'It wasn't my fault she died. Nor did I ought to really blame the lads for her death, because they couldn't help coming into the world the way they was. Though I feel bitter at times . . . Anyone would. I took up taxidermy when she went – got just about every bird as ever visits the Head pinned up here on my walls, Mister . . . Though I haven't got a roseate tern, which is uncommon scarce these days . . .'

He managed this speech with another comic face, giving me another wink and a jerk of the head as he changed the subject away from his dead wife, almost as if he were making fun of himself. The effect was somehow as sinister as it was ludicrous, and I directed his attention to the contract.

We went through the document carefully, Howe showing himself to be less foolish than his gauche social manner suggested. In my profession, I am accustomed to dealing with people who live solely for money. Albert Howe, I discerned, was indifferent to it; he wanted a fair future for his sons and believed he had secured one; the question of remuneration was a minor one to him. This factor alone set him apart from ninety per cent of the population.

As he signed the copies of the contract, the daughter appeared again, wearing a torn plastic apron over her jeans. She began to clear the table.

'The boys are ready, Dad,' she said. She sniffed as if she had been weeping.

'Come forth, lads, don't be shy!' called Howe, jerking his head.

The dog barked in the kitchen, and Tom and Barry came forth.

Contrary to my expectations, the twins were conveyed to London without difficulty. They loitered on the way to the jetty but raised no objection to climbing into Stebbings' boat when it arrived. They waved farewell to their sister in rather a perfunctory fashion.

As previously arranged, the car awaiting me at Deepdale Staithe conveyed us straight to London; I surmised that a rail journey might have its difficulties. Apart from visits to hospital and one appearance on a medical programme on BBC TV (the appearance which had inspired Zak Bedderwick to sign them up), the Howe twins had scarcely left L'Estrange Head, never mind Norfolk, until now. The journey passed without incident. They were interested in everything, especially when we entered the environs of London. It was dark when I deposited them at Zak Bedderwick's flat.

The car then drove me to my own apartment, where I was glad to take a sherry and a warm bath, and play myself Telemann sonatas.

Zak Bedderwick was every inch a business man. He was

successful in the competitive world of pop music, and would have been equally successful in banking or oil. As such, he was in my opinion a rarity. Most of the big names in his field can grasp neither their own business nor rock-and-roll. At this time, there was nobody to rival his flair or the range of his activities.

He had appointed a manager by the name of Nick Sidney to concentrate on the Howe twins and lick them into promotable shape. The twins stayed in Zak's flat overnight and no longer. The next morning, Nick Sidney arrived promptly at ten o'clock and took them down to Humbleden. I doubt if Zak ever saw them personally after that occasion; like everyone else, he had a morbid curiosity to inspect Siamese twins at first hand; once that curiosity was satisfied, his interest was purely financial.

The rest of the story hardly involves me. Bedderwick Walker was not my only concern, and at this period I became increasingly involved with a lawsuit pending over the nefarious actions of a certain Foreign Affairs Minister of a certain African state.

In any case, little news filtered out of Humbleden. Humbleden had been designed for that end.

Humbleden was one of Zak's country places. It was a grand Georgian mansion (with part of an earlier Tudor manor still preserved) standing in two hundred acres of ground with its own private lake and airstrip and a view across the Solent. What went on there was nobody's business. All the same, rumours trickled out.

Nick Sidney's training methods were known to be rather rigorous. He was a man in his late thirties, thick-set and running slightly to fat, with a shock of greasy curly hair. He had been a second division football team manager before becoming first a disc jockey and then part of Zak Bedderwick's entourage.

Sidney went to work immediately on the Howe twins. He got them cleaned up and groomed and suitably dressed, and christened them officially with their professional name, the Bang-Bang. Tom and Barry Bang-Bang.

Musical training commenced the day after they arrived at Humbleden. There were one or two second-string Bedderwick groups which Sidney could have used for backing. Instead, he chose a heavier group, the Noise, then being led by the guitarist and songwriter, Paul Day.

The Noise was in some disarray. Morale was low ever since its leader, Chris Dervish, committed suicide by driving his Charger Daytona into Datchet Reservoir immediately following a Noise concert in the Albert Hall. The Noise wanted a new image and a new direction; the Bang-Bang wanted a new noise. The two went together.

Nick Sidney had virtually built the Noise and their multi-million dollar success story, as well as Gibraltar before that, and he set to work with a will on licking his new team into shape. He had to begin at the beginning, by teaching the Howe twins to play a few basic chords on guitar and to project their singing voices. Fortunately, the twins – like every other youngster on the globe – were familiar with the conventions of pop. They disliked being prisoners of Humbleden; they had no objection to becoming prisoners of fame.

Their rages, their frequent outbreaks of recalcitrance, were dealt with by Nick Sidney with the zest he had shown towards Nottingham Albion. On the one end of the scale, he employed cold water hoses and a new-fangled electronic stun-gun; on the other, he employed the more traditional lures where pop groups were concerned, the three D's of the trade, drugs, drink and dollies.

Despite these inducements, progress was slow. I saw Zak on one occasion, just after he had returned from what he always termed 'the Manor'. Zak was quietly fuming at the lack of response from the Howe twins. I recommended sending for the sister, Robbie or Roberta, of whom the twins were obviously fond, to see if that improved matters, but

Zak brushed the suggestion aside. He wanted the Bang-Bang to sink themselves into their new roles, not to be reminded of the old ones. A preliminary tour for the Bang-Bang, on a Northern circuit and with a tie-in with Scottish television, was already scheduled for a few months ahead. As far as Bedderwick Walker were concerned, the operation had to start earning back its investment as soon as possible – any refinements to the act could come later, etc., etc. Of course I had listened to similar talk many times before. Training hooligans to bellow and strum was nothing new in the music business. Nor was failing to do so necessarily an obstacle to a profitable career.

But the day came when my gogglephone gonged and Zak's face looked out at me, voicing a new complaint.

'Henry, hi. You know of a magazine called *Sense and Society*?'

'I do. One of the Humanistic Sanity group of magazines. Left wing, of course. Circulation not more than 25,000 a month. Influential among middle-of-road socialist circles, you might say. What of it?'

'I've just had an anonymous phone call. *Sense and Society* have time-tabled for future publication an article on the exploitation of teenagers by the middle-aged, treating them as another underprivileged minority. The article will instance pop groups and make particular mention of the use of freaks to attract live audiences, complete with details of cruel training methods, including use of electronic weapons. How do we stop them?'

'That shouldn't be difficult. Humanistic Sanity depend for their liquidity on voluntary contributions, including a substantial one from the Borghese Tobacco Corporation, who happen to be clients of ours. Will the information in this proposed article come within appreciable distance of being accurate?"

'That's what I'm afraid of. It's being written up by a woman.'

'I'm sure you can manage that better than I.'

'This isn't just a dolly, Henry. She's old. Thirty-five. You know her name. Laura Ashworth. Dervish's girlfriend. Daughter of the clergyman who was in the news a few years ago.'

'I recall.'

'She's a contributor to *Sense and Society* or whatever the damned thing's called. You know how she hates me, silly bitch. If she lets out some of the murkier details – particularly if she links the Bang-Bang's name with Chris Dervish – as well she might – then our goose is cooked just as our publicity machine gets into gear. Ashworth could do us a moderate amount of damage. I want you to get her off our necks.'

While he was making threatening noises, I was thinking. Laura Ashworth was an emotional woman. She thought reasonably clearly until her adrenalin started flowing. There were ways of getting it flowing again which could guarantee she never wrote her article.

'I don't see why we should have to trouble the Borghese Tobacco Corporation, Zak. You have trouble with the Howe twins and you have trouble with Ashworth. Why not put the two sides together and see if the problems don't iron themselves out? I suggest you entice Ashworth on to your payroll and despatch her forthwith to Humbleden. She will not be able to resist the chance of reliving some of her former glories.'

That was how it worked out. Ashworth accepted Zak's offer. Whatever her intentions were about discovering 'the truth' about Humbleden – which she knew from Chris Dervish's time – may never be revealed. A friend of mine wrote a letter to the editor of *Sense and Society* asking him if he knew that one of his female contributors had taken up employment with a right-wing organization with considerable interests in the Bedderwick Development Corporation, whose exploitation of black labour in Africa and Sri Lanka was well known. Miss Ashworth's connection with that journal was speedily terminated.

In Laura Ashworth's background lay an involved story which I have no intention of relating here. Suffice it to say that she was the only daughter of a Church of England clergyman who later abandoned the cloth, and that she had no real place in society. She was one of those drifters our age so characteristically throws up. Equally characteristically, she gravitated towards the pop world – one of those homes for drifters where the inmates have taken over the asylum.

At one time, Laura Ashworth had held a post in a Department of Abnormal Psychology in a northern polytechnic, after which she had qualified as a prison probationer attached to an open prison – another home for society's drifters. Whilst at the prison, she had encountered Chris Dervish, who was there serving a sentence for drug-smuggling: a considerable quantity of heroin from Bahrein.

It was at this stage of her life that Ashworth got herself divorced from her college professor husband, one Charlie Rickards, reverted to her maiden name, and devoted herself to Dervish. When Dervish emerged from prison – and of course his stretch in the nick merely enhanced the glamour of his image with his particular public – he reformed the Noise and went on two extravagantly successful tours of the States and Scandinavia. Ashworth went with him. As her enemies liked to point out, Ashworth was almost exactly twice Dervish's age. But she had stamina. She survived Los Angeles and Stockholm and all the godless cities in between, and lived to return with him to the relative peace of Humbleden when the tours were over. I was always mystified as to how she avoided finishing up in Datchet Reservoir with him.

Some claimed that Ashworth's influence on Dervish had a stabilizing effect, others that it was she who drove him to take his life. Nick Sidney informed me that she had a disruptive effect on the Noise as a group, by which I took him to mean merely that she was particular with whom she slept. Be all that as it may, and it is pointless to bring charges where evidence is incomplete, Dervish was a psychotic from the word Go. For all his rant before the microphones, in private he was an inadequate little wet. Which made Datchet Reservoir a not unsuitable terminus for his existence, whether or not Ashworth was involved.

How the members of the group would take to her reappearance, I had no means of judging. That was not my problem. The vital thing at this juncture was that she should not raise any adverse publicity concerning the Bang-Bang in the media, when Zak's plans were maturing. I let Zak get on with it and returned to my African lawsuit. He was running the freak-show, not I.

The tale of corruption in high places which I was investigating was not then public knowledge. A few newspapers had begun to leak circumspect stories dealing with one aspect or another of the scandal : some charges facing a British Cabinet Minister, the dismissal of the head of an international contracting firm, the disappearance of a well-known architect. The trial still lay some months ahead when I was flown out to the West African state of Kanzani on behalf of Beauchamp-Fielding Associates. I was able to question some Kanzani politicians. The Minister of Health himself drove me out secretly to the chief item of evidence in the case.

Fifty kilometres from the nearest river, two hundred and fifty kilometres from any township worthy of the name, we arrived at our destination in the bush. There stood a great disconsolate white building, its tiers of windows shuttered like closed eyes, its portico already in a state of collapse. This was the multi-million dollar hospital built merely to line the pockets of a few avaricious men. The main structure had been completed. Nearby, the foundations of an X-ray unit lay open to the sky. Goats wandered about the builders' rubble.

I walked through room after room, ward after ward, all deathly quiet. No healing would ever take place here. There was no way in which one penny of the investment could be retrieved. Only the termites would benefit.

When I flew back from Nairobi, it was to find that the Bang-Bang had taken off and their first single was already in the charts.

> *I walk left, I walk right,*
> *I waste no sleeping on the night –*
> *It's two by two, the light the dark*
> *Just like animals in the Ark*
> *Because I'll tell ya*
> *Tell ya*
> *I'm a Two-Way Romeo*
>
> *Hatched right under that Gemini sign*
> *Magic number Sixty-Nine*
> *We're two in one and all in all*
> *Shoot double-barrelled wherewithal ...*
>
> *Girls cumma my house, I let 'em in,*
> *I say Wait, I say Begin –*
> *At first it's strange but then it lives*
> *They grow to love the alternatives*
> *'N' then they'll tell ya*
> *Tell ya*
>
> *I'm a Two-Way Romeo*
> *Bang-Bang*
> *A Two-Way Thru-Way New-Way Romeo*[1]

Looking back, one is astonished to recall the fury which accompanied the success of this execrable song. On their first Northern tour, the Howe twins appeared as support to another of Zak's groups. Their gig, as I understand the term to be, was closed down in Sunderland for reasons of indecency; with Zak's financial backing, the manager of the Sunderland club contested this decision in the courts, and the affair was given some publicity. From then on, a trail of accusations of indecency and innuendo followed like exhaust fumes in the wake of the Bang-Bang's speeding career.

A question was soon raised in the Houses of Parliament. National debate followed, to the strains of that tuneless song. Should the physiologically deprived make capital of their deprivation? Was it fair to themselves and their public?

We can see now why the Bang-Bang was difficult to take. At the time, much of the discussion centred on whether their songs and performances were good or bad; in fact, the question of art hardly entered into the matter. The question of morality was a good deal more pressing (but the British public is well accustomed to confusing art with morality).

Two overlapping areas of morality served to make the Bang-Bang hot news. The Bang-Bang were Siamese twins and therefore represented a deformity (for libel reasons, the word 'freak' was rarely used in public); should deformity be exploited in this way – indeed, *was* it being exploited?

And – this was the more painful area – should deformed people be allowed to flaunt their sexuality? The deformed, the handicapped, were supposed to keep quiet about their natural desires. There was enough material here to keep the pot of virtuous sentiment, seasoned with prurient interest, a-boiling for a long while.

Self-appointed guardians of the country's moral fibre claimed that sexuality and music were being debased, that national sensitivities would suffer. Then a Liberal Member of Parliament went on television to state that, in his humble opinion, it was all to the good that minorities such as Siamese twins should have their voice; and moreover that his family (although not he himself) had greatly enjoyed the energy of the Bang-Bang, as well as the pagan innocence of their songs. He considered them good-looking young men. He did not see anything unpleasant in deformity, and looked forward to the day when greater enlightenment brought multiple sclerosis olympics and similar events.

This speech was so widely reported, with further photographs of the Bang-Bang and other deformed people who had immediately sought to cash in on the Bang-Bang's success, that it drove out the news of two more African states, including Kanzani, being overtaken by Communist coups.

Debated, photographed, interviewed, booked solid, the Bang-Bang rose immediately from strength to strength.

Imitating their rough Norfolk accents became a national pastime among the young. Deformity became chic. Fake Siamese twins became the rage. Singing amputees appeared on the Palladium bill.

It was stardust from then on for the Howe twins: the usual vulgar story of success. Talk of wrecked hotel rooms, hysterical female fans, drink, and strong-arm bodyguards eager to do their stuff, only added to the excitement. The triumphal tours made in this country were transferred to the United States with even greater success, then to Europe, then to other parts of the globe. There was the special Concorde flight to Kuwait, the launching of Bang-Bang magazines, a raft of golden discs, and, inevitably, the constant flow of money and more money, unstaunchable, like blood pouring down a drain.

Even in the grotesque annals of the rock industry, the Bang-Bang provided one of those fabulous stories which appeared too good to be true. Certainly it was too good to last. The celebrated film director, Saul Spielbaum, made a film with the Bang-Bang and Laura Ashworth (inevitably called *Two-Way Romeo*), with surrealist trappings;

29

execrated by the critics, its takings exceeding such previous legends of the cinema as *Close Encounters*, the James Bond films, *Jaws*, and *The Executioner's Beautiful Daughter*.

Into this story, as sticky with success as a treacle tart, the question of art scarcely seems to enter. The Bang-Bang sang no better and no worse than many other young ruffians who have made a fortune with a microphone, a glittering suit, and a few rudimentary pelvic gestures. Their music was technically indistinguishable from other music of the period. But they were unique. They did appear to be 'two in one and all in all'.

Always behind the brouhaha pulsed a vein of morbid curiosity. It ran through the youngest fan as through the commentators and culture experts who used the example of the Bang-Bang to spice up their own theories. For the Bang-Bang was not a solo singer; nor was it a pop group; it was Siamese twins. And the twins' first and most perennial song – as Zak Bedderwick had calculated – provoked the ever-interesting question: what was their sex-life like?

CHAPTER 2

Laura Ashworth's Report

Having suffered from years of snide innuendo, I will open my contribution to this book by declaring that my attitude towards Tom and Barry was non-exploitive. It started non-exploitive and it stayed that way. They were in an exploitive situation and everyone got all tangled up in it. So much fame just drives you out of your mind. The pressures are too great. After our first USA tour, Tom and Barry and I ran away one day, and we found a field full of big white daisies. We just rolled in them. The boys began a fight over something, but I stopped them. We were so happy that we started singing. I picked some daisies. Tom said he would buy me the whole field. Barry said he would buy it, he would pay more. They started betting how much they would pay for the field, how they would build a dome over it and have daisies grow there all year long. At first we were laughing.

Then they said how good it would be to convey the field around everywhere on tour with us. They discussed how it could be done, how much money it would take. I suddenly felt the field was not real any more. It had turned into a status symbol, an item of cash flow, another cause of rancour between the brothers. I did not want the field and, even if I did, I would never see it again. Even if I saw it again, I could never be free in it again. I got up and walked back to our helicopter. They followed and we never said another word until we were far away.

Well, it is impossible to be free and very difficult to be happy. I had a trendy sociologist friend – had being the operative word, because fame loses you friends faster than failure – who wrote about us. He took the easy line that the Bang-Bang were victims of capitalist society. It was the sort of thing my father would have said. It was a fashionable, superficial, smarty-pants thing to say. The truth was that we were victims of society's pent-up secret wishes. The capitalist world has no monopoly on pent-up secret wishes. Everyone everywhere suffers from shortage of opportunity to fulfil their whole selves: it's just that *we're* allowed to grumble about the situation. That was what made Tom and Barry so madly attractive – they were like one person with double capacity.

Enough philosophy. Before I go into *us*, I will start with an outline of myself, the kind of girl I am, right or wrong, and what made me that way.

I was the only girl in a family with four brothers. They were all older than I. My mother died when I was in my teens. Funnily enough, I know I should miss her a great deal but somehow I hardly recall her. I do recall the vicarage where we lived, though. I suppose it was dark and awful, but I loved it. The rooms were like jungles. I was a little wild beast.

During mother's long illness, I grew closer to father, especially as my brothers left home. Father was vicar of a poor London parish south of the river. He was always working. He never relaxed. Something drove him. He was always 'kind' in a hasty way, rather as if my brothers and I were favoured members of the parish.

Mother was a hard worker too. Vicars' wives were chosen for work capacity, not virtuosity in bed or anything like that. She and father brought me up as rather a bluestocking. This sounds madly old-fashioned and eccentric but we had no television panel, and mother used to read aloud to me and my brothers. Once she read all of Winwood Reade's *The Martyrdom of Man*, which is quite an anti-religious book. And father sat in the corner, writing, writing, at his bureau, with his back to the light. He wrote gothic fantasies under the name of Nikola McLaren. Some of them are good. I re-read *Nightingale Summer* recently and quite enjoyed it. In fact, I wept a bit because I thought that I as a little girl had served as model for the girl in the book who is kidnapped by the gipsies.

My father's fantasies helped to pay for my further education. I can see I owe him a lot, but I wonder if he was not too negative to be called a good man. He believed in all the things that intelligent middle-class people believed in during the sixties. He believed in equality between the sexes (practically forcing me to join Women's Lib, which I loathed), in cutting government defence spending, in the abolition of all colour bars and racial discrimination (he almost coerced me into the arms of any black who wandered into the vicarage), better and more education for the poorer classes, unlimited assistance for all the scroungers of our society, vast aid programmes for the Third World, severing of diplomatic relations with South Africa (but not a word against the Soviet Union). And so on. From which you will gather that my father was also for the abolition of private cars, non-returnable bottles, beer cans, plastics of all sorts, meat-eating, tobacco, advertising, and almost all forms of alcohol, wine excepted – in short, almost anything that helps an ordinary citizen lead something less than a dog's life.

As you will readily understand, in politics my father was a watered-down Marxist. I only once saw him in a genuine rage, when someone called him 'a bloody left-wing intellectual'. He preferred to think of himself as 'practising liberalism with a small "l" ', as he once put it – 'not unlike our Lord himself'.

My father claimed to believe that the working classes had never had a chance – a chance for what he never went on to specify. He was also intensely patriotic, so much so that it influenced what taste he had in music. He once published a pamphlet on John Earle, a seventeenth-century bishop in whom he took an interest. The improving conversations which went along with our frugal vicarage meals in my childhood centred round the three Deadly E's, as I thought of them, Engels, Elgar and Earle.

Despite this dreary catalogue of virtues, I did love my father. I loved him in a sort of angry, admiring, pitying despair. He believed all that he believed in simply because that was what it was fashionable to believe. Or rather because that was what people in his class had believed a few years earlier. I can still blush with shame when I recall how he conducted a service one Sunday wearing jeans. Poor father! I used to argue savagely with him – simply because I hoped that he might by argument come to believe in his heart what he really only professed to believe. It seemed to me that in his heart there was no belief at all.

'You'll see how things are in the world when you are older, my dear. And that will be time enough,' he would say.

'Father, you are as sheltered from the world by your beliefs as I am.'

'My parish is to me a microcosm of the world. Its errors and aspirations are the world's.'

'You know nothing about your parish, nothing—'

'I can't let you say that, Laura,' my mother would interrupt. 'Your dear father has dedicated his life to the poor of this down-trodden stretch of London for over twenty years—'

'Oh, I know, mother, but you, neither of you see what you call the poor as they really are. It's all theory with you. Theory is everything to you. You don't give a bugger about the actual people.'

'Now, my dear child, you mustn't allow yourself to talk like that. You'll only regret it later.'

I felt even his patience with me was insincere; now, now, I'm much less sure of everything.

But it was true that he understood nothing about other people. Perhaps that was why he wrote fantasies (of which of course he was ashamed). He did live and work with 'the poor of the parish', but they knew how to protect themselves

34

from this sort of cant. *I* knew those people. I played with them, I went into their homes.

Most of them didn't care a scrap for anything beyond their own families, their own cronies, their own selves, their own wage packet. They elbowed their way through life independent of all theories. I admired them for that – and hated them for it. I was working through psychology and psychoanalysis, those King Rat's palaces of theory.

Year after year, through my childhood and growing-up, father laboured in what he sometimes referred to as his vineyard, never understanding why he did not make contact with his flock.

He had sense enough to perceive that he had failed, that Ma Jones and Shamus O'Leary did not give a hoot about the plight of the workers in poor oppressed Panama or the starving multitudes in Bangladesh. What he could not understand was that he himself had never felt the bite of real Christianity. I was a Christian once, and it hurt too much. I gave it up. I saw my father was preaching hogwash. I hated him then.

The day came when something went wrong. Just one more small discouragement. He said that people did not look up to him any more. He went upstairs to see mother in her sick-bed. I stood downstairs in the hall and listened to him weeping on the other side of her closed door. I felt so ashamed, loitering among the plastic macs and anoraks. After lunch, which he missed, father came down pale and shaky and pushed his bicycle out of the porch. He cycled off to see his bishop and throw up his ministry.

Of course, he still had to stick around with theology because he knew nothing else. He got a staff job in a Midlands theological college. It meant the final break-up of our family, because the vicarage had to go (they demolished it and the next incumbent had a trendy flat above Hair Flair in the new shopping centre). I know father bitterly regretted all that, yet I did not care what he felt at the time. He was

35

always so 'kind' to me, whatever that means. Kindness was another of his theories.

That was a desperate sort of period. Everything fell apart. While father was busy renouncing his ministry, mother died. I had been nursing her while working for my exams. I used to get up at six every morning, under the firm impression that everyone in vicarages always got up at six every morning. None of my brothers was much help – only one of them even lived in London.

The night that mother died, father was out, chairing a damned Save the Sick committee. I left her where she lay and went out into the street. I just felt ghastly, blank, sick.

A few metres down the street, I bumped into Ricky Hayes. Ricky was a young Jamaican, one of father's lost sheep. A bastard but with a great sense of fun – something as rare as the crown jewels in our household. I seized on him, begged him to buy me a drink – I never had any money – and then make love to me. So he did, so he did. Nobody exploited anybody, and everybody was happy. I desperately needed what he had got.

And instead of losing interest afterwards, Ricky, who had a lot of girls, kindly took me along to see Chris Dervish and the Noise. He knew the drummer. It was great, and not a bit like life at the vicarage. The din was intoxicating.

Dervish was not so well-known then. Ricky took me backstage afterwards to say hello to Chris. Ricky was sexy but Dervish was just psychotic. He started to make demands of me then, right in front of the others. That also was not like life in the vicarage, but I didn't knock it on that account. Though I could see what a mixed-up guy Dervish was.

That story the papers kept repeating about my meeting Dervish when he was in prison was untrue. Reporters just crib off old press cuttings. Chris was so wild, so frightened under everything. He was longing for a nice quiet open prison like Parkhurst, where he landed up after his Middle East adventure.

I felt protective towards Chris, even when he was exploiting me for all he was worth. He was younger than me. I wept and wept when he drowned himself in the reservoir. I would probably have killed myself too, if it had not been for an old friend of mine at the clinic where I worked. (He was a man called Charlie Rickards, and I was never married to him, as some reporters claimed.)

Yet it wasn't really Chris who turned me on. The music did that. I just dug rock. The past ceased to exist for me, and the future, when Chris was up there playing. Maybe it was the amplification, or the sexual ranting, or the whole atmosphere of demented licence. I don't know what it was. I just know it wasn't one fucking bit like the vicarage. I was gone.

The whole ethos of pop is classless working-class. It's naïve and uncritical and inarticulate. Nobody knows what they are doing but sometimes they feel what they are doing. And sometimes they do it right. Way behind it lies black jazz and that too came from another sort of 'free jungle', as Dervish once described it. There's a feeling of native tribes, of ritualization – something much more powerful than words and music.

All that I felt – oh, yes, I felt it, and at first all I wanted to do was to hear the sounds and get laid. But my upbringing saw to it that a divided part of myself also enjoyed the feeling that I was rejecting good taste and the whole dreary Christian-Imperial tradition dying the death elsewhere in the country. No phoney 'kindness' here, just genuine raw feeling. Maybe much of it looked vile from outside, and it was often hard to take, but in its reality it seemed pure to me. At least at first. Some bad things happened to me at Humbleden in Dervish's day which it is better should remain buried.

Chris Dervish's suicide made me see life was not as simple as I had tried to pretend. Undisciplined feeling killed him. He could not cope with it. Many other people would have gone down in his position, adulated but a captive of that adulation.

That chapter of life was closed by the time I met Tom and Barry Howe. I drove myself down to Humbleden in my Mini. It was a lovely August afternoon. Although I was no foolish virgin, I did not know what I was getting into.

Humbledon I knew and loved. I liked its style. It stood for a self-assurance, a fine sense of established values, which you had to admire. The house was beautifully sited on a slight rise, with its lake, the work of Capability Brown, lying before it. Through the line of great cedars on the south side of the lake were glimpses of the sea, the vital sea where you could be a child again. Wave-sparkle flew into my eyes, blinking between moving cedar trunks as I drove up. Organic life moved too – swans, ducks, deer in the park, horses in a paddock, never ridden and restless in fly-tormented shade. What was it all but the fruit of 'privilege', that word my poor father could not pronounce without pursing his lips? I never subscribed to the notion that all men were equal, or not after the first time I went with Ricky. Besides, what did under-privilege build one half so handsome and enduring?

It was quiet inside the house that afternoon. Quiet, except for the sound of rock from a distant room. No one about. The guy that ran the place, Nick Sidney, was typically not to be found. Not that I felt any great rush to see him again.

In the kitchens, I found Tubby Puller, the Noise drummer, scoffing sandwiches. He greeted me without interest, as if he had seen me only the day before, and told me that 'the freaks' were up in their suite on the second floor. I climbed the stairs. Still emptiness. Loud grabby rock issued from what used to be the art gallery on the first floor. It pleased me that I could recognize Paul Day's guitar.

On the second floor, the house became meaner, the corridor narrower, the rooms smaller. This had been the servants' floor in the old days.

I walked along the corridor. Someone was playing an

38

electric guitar badly. When I came to the appropriate door, I knocked and marched in.

I had done a fair amount of research on Tom and Barry for my article for *Sense and Society*, and knew what there was to know about them. I had not met them. My first impression was of confusion – and something else, not quite horror, not quite terror, almost awe.

They were too close. They were always a crowd. They grew together like two trees growing where only one should be, branches hopelessly intertwined, distorting each other.

That was my first impression – one of entanglement. So wild were they, that they leapt up as soon as I entered. I had only an impression of their previous attitude, with Barry sitting on the swelling curve of a Victorian sofa arm while Tom attempted to sprawl beside him. Barry was plucking a guitar while Tom tried to read a paperback book. Their elbows got in each other's way. The thought crossed my mind that both guitar-playing and reading were so foredoomed to failure that they were glad of the diversion I caused.

But it was not like that. They were genuinely wild, backing away from me like untrusting dogs. They were joined to each other just below the shoulder and at the hip. On Barry's other shoulder was that other head, leaning forward in an attitude of sleep.

'What do you want?' Barry asked.

'I'm a new member of Zak's staff. Hello. The name's Laura Ashworth, and I could use a drink.'

'Pub's down the road,' said Tom. They stood on guard, weighing me up, and I countered with my own curious stare. You could not help staring. There was a compulsion to stare.

The twins were strapping young men of eighteen, not fourteen or fifteen as some accounts have claimed. Tension marked them. Barry was more sturdily built than his brother; he had a red peasant face, complete with snub nose

39

and startling light grey eyes which generally regarded you through half-closed lids, as if he were tired, or dangerous, or forever summing you up. His thatch of thick black hair stood up spikily from his low forehead. Tom was not so thick-set and looked slightly taller, though he carried his head to one side. His face was less flushed and thinner than his brother's. The hair that curled attractively about his neck and ears was a nondescript brown. He appeared more vulnerable than his brother. While he offered me a tentative smile, his brother scowled. There was a sensuous expression about Tom's lips, I thought.

Looking back, I can no longer be sure of first impressions. I was full of a sort of terror. Though I immediately felt their differences, I was also conscious of their blanket similarity, caused by their inseparable state.

Yet that head dozing on Barry's shoulder set them apart. It made Barry the deformed twin, as well as the one with power. On that first meeting, I scarcely dared look at it. Afterwards, my glances were always covert – although the fact that it has lain on a pillow against my head makes me as familiar with it as the next person.

The third head seemed to have no relation to Tom or Barry. It lay in repose on Barry's left shoulder, nodding forward. Barry always held his head away from it, which caused Tom to carry his head straining slightly to the right, so that he always looked at you slightly awry. The third head was small. It appeared to belong to an old man; its features were withered, its hair grey. Its eyes were closed, the eye-sockets sunken. Later I saw how greatly it resembled Barry's face, despite its pallor, which contrasted with his ruddiness.

'I thought you'd offer me a drink,' I said.

'We're going out,' said Barry.

A struggle took place between them, though neither changed position. It was a battle of wills, of impulses, of hesitations, expressed in tensed muscles, clenched fists. Barry took a step forward.

'We're going *out*,' he said.

Then they were like liquid. The struggle was over, they ran forward with uncanny co-ordination, four legs complexly moving, as they passed me and headed for the door. In a moment they were gone. As they reached the stairs, they gave a strange united yell, a noise that might have been fear or derision or exultation.

I stood in their room, listening to the sounds of their descent through the house until it was drowned by the music. I was shaken. For a moment, I had thought they were going to attack me. But it was more than that. Their presence had been a challenge to my own being.

At last I turned. Before I reached the door, a movement through the windows caught my eye. The twins were out there.

I went over and looked down. Still running, they had crossed the drive to the paddock. Lightly, they vaulted together over the fence to where four hunters stood in the shade of spreading oaks. They formed one figure when they ran – that was when their unity was most sharply expressed. No two ordinary people could run that close.

The horses backed away. The twins did not pause. Grabbing a mane, they launched themselves up and were astride in no time. It looked from where I was as if each had a leg on either side of the animal's back. Before I could be sure, they had kicked the horse into action and were off, galloping madly away, parallel to the white fence, dashing through sun and shadow.

Having gone into much detail about my first encounter with the twins, and how that first encounter came about, I find myself in difficulty about proceeding. What happened between Tom and me, and between Barry and me, is private.

It may sound funny for a journalist to say that, but I do think that the more details I fill in, the less the magic of what happened will be recaptured. Because I did come to love them both.

An outline it will have to be. A silhouette. The twins got to know me. I stayed unobtrusive, attending their music lessons and the afternoon sessions with the group, and talking to people they were talking to, like Paul Day, the Noise's guitarist, for whom I had always had respect. I chugged round the lake in Zak's launch with them, I went on the beach with them, I even rode a horse for their sake – though not bareback. Some of it was fun. More often, it was pain.

There was so much hatred. Nick Sidney treated the twins as freaks; he had a special weapon – a stun-gun – to deal with them, as if he were a wild animal trainer. He had established a pecking order in the manor. The members of the Noise were accommodated as he was, in luxurious rooms on the first floor. When I was offered a similar room, I refused it and took an attic room in the servants' quarters, where the twins were exiled. They were supposed to eat alone.

Of course, they were rough country lads. But that was not the trouble. The trouble was that they hated Nick, they hated the Noise, they hated each other. They hated their distant father for 'selling them', as they put it.

But they enjoyed the singing. They liked to bellow and stamp and project themselves. They wished to be the Bang-Bang and to rant and caper before screaming audiences. This wish was so strong that they submitted to Nick Sidney, up to a point. Training sessions were alarming feats of antagonism, with the Noise rebellious, hating the Bang-Bang and trying to outplay them. In trying to hold it all in one piece, Sidney drank more than ever and used his fists when he felt like it.

The exception to all this antagonism was Paul Day, who rode along with it as if enjoying the storms. He had become a lot more together since the days of Dervish.

42

Even the sessions failed to unite Tom and Barry. They found it impossible to play guitar together. Their tensions destroyed their sense of unison. Fights broke out, instruments were destroyed. Tom was really not a fighter, although he fought his brother savagely in self-defence. Barry might have been wrestling with a devil. He fought Tom, he fought the Noise, he fought anyone who came within range, including Nick Sidney. Sidney fought back; Sidney used his stun-gun.

After one hellish struggle, Barry hit Sidney behind the ear with the edge of an electric guitar and laid him out cold. The twins ran, and were later seen perched on the roof of Humbleden, crouching by a chimney-stack. When I stood in the courtyard and called to them to come down, Barry flung a tile at me.

Some days later, after another violent scene, I phoned Zak Bedderwick. We had never been on particularly good terms, but he was civil enough. I respected him more than he did me; surprisingly enough, he knew a fair bit about music. I asked him if he would summon a qualified surgeon to come and give the twins a thorough examination.

'I know what's on your mind,' he said. 'You'd better forget it. They can't be separated and that's final. Besides, if they were separated, we wouldn't have an act.'

'You may not have an act as it is. They are all set to destroy everything. Look, Zak, I know something about their sort of mentality, and they are in pain – mental pain, right? Get another medical opinion. Maybe you could offer them separation in five years if they co-operate now. That could be the only way. Otherwise, someone could get killed.'

'You really go for that kind of drama, Sunshine, don't you?'

But he gave in and sent a surgeon to Humbleden.

Zak may have suspected that I was in some way going to get him adverse publicity if a surgeon arrived, since a surgeon could be said to emphasize the medical oddity of

Tom and Barry. Although I feared for the mental stability of the twins, I had already given up any idea of writing them up as objects of exploitation. I sensed in them, as in Chris Dervish before them, a blind urge to be exploited. They wanted the world to know of them. I was not going to make theory fit reality, as my father would have done.

The surgeon was Sir Allardyce Stevens. He was a small dapper man in his late sixties, with pale translucent skin and light eyes. He looked as if you could blow him over, and his smile was the gentlest thing I had ever seen. I feared for him in the presence of the terrible twins, yet they became as docile as lambs as soon as they saw him. What they hoped for from him was, I suppose, obvious enough. Sir Allardyce was a man to inspire hope.

He was with the twins for more than two hours.

He talked to me afterwards. Much of what he said was technical and over my head, but the gist of it was clear. Tom and Barry were conjoined twins, joined by ligament from breastbone to hip, in the manner of the original Siamese twins. Their circulatory systems communicated and, as is apparently typical in trunk fusions, they shared organs, including kidneys and other minor bits and pieces I had never heard of.

I felt flattered by Sir Allardyce's careful explanation and his assumption that I cared. I took him for a drink before his chauffeur drove him back to London. He went into medical details about how surgery was still not advanced enough to separate the two of them and have them both live. There were reasonable guarantees that one would live but not both.

'Which one?' I asked.

'That would have to be decided, my dear,' he said, sipping his brandy and tonic and smiling at me. 'Speaking as a surgeon, I would prefer to see Tom survive. Theirs is an unusual case. Superficially, they are symmetrical twins, as were Chang and Eng, the original pair. But Barry himself forms a host or autosite member of a secondary twinning. That extraordinary head on his shoulder forms an undeveloped parasite. It represents a third twin, a triplet or the beginning of one, as you might say, and is dependent on Barry, its host, for nutrition.'

'A parasite! Is it alive? Couldn't you operate and remove it?'

He pursed his lips. 'I wouldn't care to be the one to try; there are too many random factors. At birth, it would have been a different matter. As for the question of *life* in the parasite, well, not only that . . .'

He hesitated.

'Go on.'

'Barry is not a communicative lad, as you know. But he said an odd thing to me. I questioned him about the head – for which he has a name, by the way. Significant, that. He wouldn't tell me the name, and I didn't press him. He feels protective about it. He said that he relies on the third head.'

'Relies on it? How?'

'He's just a simple Norfolk lad. His attitude is partly superstitious.'

'But is the head . . . alive?'

'Certainly it is alive, or otherwise decomposition would have set in long ago. A more pertinent question concerns cerebral activity. Apparently that question was not considered during previous examinations. The eyes are permanently closed, but I observed REM activity.'

'What's REM?'

'Rapid Eye Movement. Suggesting strongly that the third head is in a dreaming state.'

We were sitting in the bar on the ground floor, in what had once been the library. All books had long ago disappeared. There were some comics on one of the tables nearby. Sunshine poured through the stained glass and coloured crimson and green the carpet at our feet. There we sat,

45

having this extraordinary conversation. I hardly knew what to say.

'A dreaming state . . . You mean – the third head could wake up at any time?'

Sir Allardyce took a long sip of his drink and gazed at me as he did so. He smiled. His reassuring manner was at variance with the alarming information he was giving me.

'We are entering rather a speculative area of discussion. I do not believe it likely that the third head will "wake up", since its brain has given no indication in eighteen years that it functions normally. As far as we can tell without more rigorous examination, it has remained and will remain in a state of permanent unconsciousness.'

'Nevertheless, it is . . . a person?'

'A latent personality, certainly, yes. But destined to remain latent, unless some unexpected shock wakens it to life.'

I wanted to ask him what would happen then, but the question was too fantastic. I remained silent, trying to digest the information he had given me.

'It must be a bit creepy for Barry, come to think of it, always having that head with its closed eyes so near to you, mustn't it?' I laughed uneasily.

The laugh sounded like a giggle to me. Sir Allardyce laughed heartily in return.

'Indeed, yes, a bit creepy.'

'Perhaps that's why Tom seems the more normal of the two. He's really a dear . . . And you'd have him survive – if it ever came to an operation?'

The brandy was doing him good. He crossed his neat legs and relaxed. 'As I have said, such an operation is quite out of the question at present, except in an emergency. Modern medicine can supply simple spare parts – like artificial hearts, which are really only straightforward pumps – but we still cannot manage the complicated biological engineering which would be required in a separation, were both twins to survive such an operation.'

We were sitting closely together. I suddenly perceived that he fancied me sexually. A familiar mingling of curiosity, defensiveness, pleasure, and power came over me. He was a bit long in the tooth for that sort of thing. On the other hand, I could not help liking him very much, and admiring the qualities I sensed in his mind.

As if he appreciated the current of my feelings, he rose and bought us both another drink. We began to talk more generally.

When it was time for him to leave, he took my hand.

'Is there anything I can do for the twins?' I asked him.

He gave me a straight look which had in it both malice and humour. 'I don't know; is there?'

I looked down and saw how plump and brown my hand was between his. His were thin papery hands, marked with veins and liver spots. But there was still strength in them.

He said, 'You are beautiful, Laura, and I see formidable qualities in you. Don't get too emotionally involved with the Howes – though, heaven knows, they need someone like you. It could bring you a lot of unhappiness.'

Before I could think of an appropriate answer, he had climbed into his car. A wave of the hand and he was gone.

I went back into the bar, feeling I should have responded more adequately. I ordered another drink, then decided I had had enough.

Nick Sidney came into the bar, flushed in the face.

'There you are. Now that that bloody old queer's gone, perhaps you'll do the job you came down here to do and go and look after those bloody freaks. Didn't you hear the racket? They've been busting up the studio one more time.'

'You're an uncouth bastard, Nick,' I said, as I walked past him.

'And proud of it. How else would I survive in this shower?'

After this exchange, I proceeded upstairs. The twins had been doing a certain amount of damage, nothing serious.

They were objecting again to the way they were being treated. This anger against others turned, as it frequently did, into a fight with themselves. Barry was particularly frightening in his anger fits. His face became distorted. Even the third head, the one for which he had a secret name, took on a different appearance. The cheeks of its face flushed. I wondered if I would have noticed that detail in the general rumpus, had it not been for the conversation with Sir Allardyce.

They had a method of dealing with Barry's anger. Zak Bedderwick had provided Sidney with a Japanese-made stun-gun, as I mentioned. I never understood how it worked, except that it was electronic; when you fired it against someone's temples it switched the brain's Alpha rhythms to Delta rhythms, thus changing the wave frequency so that the victim fell into a deep sleep. This handy instrument was used to put Barry out when he was causing trouble.

This treatment became the rule throughout the whole success period of the Bang-Bang, especially on tour, when the stresses were particularly great. During the periods when Barry was unconscious I was able to talk to Tom. I grew very fond of him, despite Sir Allardyce's warning. I feared the situation and would not have had anything happen to Tom; but it was not that alone which drew me.

At the height of their success, after the Scandinavian tour, I was separated from the twins. I believe that I was a good influence on them, despite stories to the contrary. But some people, among them the lawyer, Henry Couling (a sort of self-appointed guardian to the twins, although he did nothing to help them), decided I was a cause for scandal in associating closely with both of the twins. Eventually Zak Bedderwick and Nick Sidney got rid of me. My feelings were bitter, although I knew how little personal feelings count in the pop industry.

In respect to certain aspects of this matter, on which no doubt others will offer distorted versions of the truth, I would like to say only that the drugs in the case have been exaggerated by the media. They were Sidney's idea in the first place. I came to use them reluctantly.

As for the immorality charges, understanding people will realize that Tom and Barry needed love and sex just like anyone else, and suffered from deprivation. There was a jealousy between them, as between all brothers, but, in view of their physical inseparability, it was inevitable that any woman who came close to either of them would have to make what accommodation she could to both.

I prefer not to be more explicit.

CHAPTER 3

Excerpt from taped interview with Nickolas Sidney

Interviewed by John James Loomis of the Canadian Broadcasting Authority.

JOHN JAMES LOOMIS: Now if we might move to a more controversial area, Nick, concerning the part Laura Ashworth played in the Bang-Bang's affairs.

NICKOLAS SIDNEY: No, there was nothing controversial. You know what it is, you're running a group, you're running a group. It's a business like any other, besides the Bang-Bang were, let's face it, freaks so they were more unstable than most. Only to be expected. So we did everyone a favour trying to keep women away, specially a girl like Láura, known dynamite.

J.J.L.: I have studied Laura's report on her side of the matter. She begins very openly, and gives a full account of conversations held, what everyone said, so on. Then—

N.S.: Yeah, well you know some people just can't keep their mouths shut. We could have managed everything fine—

J.J.L.: I was saying, Laura begins frankly, then suddenly there's a point she sort of closes down. Suddenly there's a funny sentence, like 'Following this conversation, I proceeded to the studio to see the damage.' Something of the sort. Conveys the impression she suddenly went impersonal and doesn't wish to commit herself to what really went on.

N.S.: Why should she? You've got to stick together, people will lie themselves blind. Look, I've got no kicks against Laura Ashworth—

J.J.L.: Excuse me but you do sound prejudiced.

N.S.: I'm not against anyone in this world. I've managed

football teams in my time, live and let live I say. She was a good girl and nice-looking too, even if she did kind of stir things up. She kept them occupied, the Bang-Bang I mean. But the things she did, I'm no toffee-nose, right, but she wouldn't want to tell it, spell it all out, couldn't expect her to. We knew what was going on, but you wouldn't want me to say it either, not over TV, a family show, we all knew about it, I know the way things are. Everyone says they were musical geniuses, so what if they were kooky as well, let's leave it at that. It's all over now, isn't it?

J.J.L.: Then perhaps we might talk about the drugs aspect, and the Japanese stun-gun.

N.S.: Okay, we had a violence problem. Barry was the dangerous one. Tom was quiet enough. You know what I mean. So we had to calm him down, Barry. The stun-gun's harmless. There isn't a strait-jacket made that would fit Siamese twins, so we gave him sweet dreams instead.

J.J.L.: My understanding is that the stun-gun is a development of the EEG, the electro-encephalograph, capable of switching the brain's activity from about ten cycles to one cycle per second, thus thrusting the victim into deep sleep. It's an illegal instrument in the West.

N.S.: About that . . . It never hurt him. See, if you injected Barry with something to lay him out, they'd both be out cold because their blood circulation circulated between them, see what I mean. We had to do something before he bust up the joint, what you expect us to do? You know what Laura called me? An uncouth something. But I was the guy who got in close. Twice I had a black eye. He laid me out cold. He was possessed when he took off that Barry real bonkers. He laid me out cold. She got some sort of a hold over them, okay, I let her borrow the gun occasionally – she put him out cold with it when it suited her purpose.

J.J.L.: An emotional hold over them?

N.S.: You know what I mean. Sex. That was all she was after. Put Barry out cold, have it off with Tom.

J.J.L.: And on the occasion when Barry regained consciousness while that was happening, there was presumably another row until she accommodated him as well?

N.S.: Look, I don't want to stir things up. Let sleeping dogs lie. Your guess is as good as mine.

J.J.L.: But you are making certain imputations against Laura Ashworth. It couldn't be, Nick, that this is prejudice speaking and that she was not guilty of such behaviour? There are rumours that in Dervish's day Laura was the victim of a mass-rape in which your name was involved. She hardly sounds the Lady Dracula type to me.

N.S.: Look, I don't want to . . . Look, who's stirring things . . . I said she was a sweet girl, din' I? What's past's past, that's my motto, and I s'pose that Paul Day's been shooting off his mouth again, Jesus. It doesn't matter now, does it? We're talking about history. It wasn't my job to stand outside their bedroom door like a bloody sentry, was it? I didn't want to know, I was their manager, not a wet nurse, don't forget.

J.J.L.: You had your orders from Zak?

N.S.: Zak was the boss. Same as Couling the lawyer said, our business is music, not morals. We aren't a bunch of kids who—

J.J.L.: Nevertheless, you feel defensive, understandably in view of what—

N.S.: You keep putting words into my head, things that were never there. I liked the boys and I liked Laura and I was only doing my job. I *made* them, I'm proud to say. Look, it's just we had a lot of crap all along, everyone exaggerating everything. It's all in the past, isn't it? You seem to forget we're talking about the greatest success story the world has ever known.

CHAPTER 4

Zak Bedderwick's narrative

We built the Bang-Bang into a great success story. Inevitably, some of us sustained bruises on the way, but that does not take away from what we achieved. Scandal still circulates about the names of Laura Ashworth and the Howe twins – inevitably, since from the start the public insisted on regarding the twins as sexual objects. My intention here is briefly to try to show how what happened between the young people involved was natural and perhaps inevitable, and how it contributed to the art of the Bang-Bang. I am not a music critic in any sense. I shall just point out what is there to be read in the lyrics as they developed.

This may be the place to admit that I may have been a little unfair to Laura Ashworth in the past. We have to be wary of permanent or semi-permanent female hangers-on because of their possible disruptive influence on our groups. But Laura was more victim than vamp or vampire, of that I am now convinced. In ways which I shall indicate, she served as vital catalyst in the success of the Bang-Bang. (I must add that because of an unstable home background she was somewhat unstable herself and some of her public utterances should be disregarded. For instance, the Bedderwick Walker organization did not dismiss her; she simply ran away from an emotional situation she could not resolve, following the Scandinavian tour.)

The other vital element in that emotional equation was Paul Day, our songwriter. He and Laura were deeply involved with each other. As can be seen from the lyrics.

Day was an undersized youth who grew up in a Northern town and was drumming with various groups by the age of fifteen. By the time he joined Gibraltar as drummer/

guitarist, he had had songs published. He became chief songwriter for the Bang-Bang, and played guitar with them.

On and off-stage Day presented great contrasts. Off-stage, it was difficult to get a word out of him; he would slink by without speaking if he could. Get him on the platform and a different persona took over. He then became a great extrovert personality; his inspired performances were highly regarded. To my personal regret, he has since left our organization and gone solo. The last I heard of him, he was working in the southern United States.

To my mind, Day's silences reflected an interior dilemma. He came from a broken home and had been wounded in the process. This led him to regard the Howe twins with sympathy from the start. Whereas they suffered from ostracism by the other members of the group.

I would like to clear Nick Sidney's name. He's a nice man and I could not do without him. But the Bang-Bang were very difficult and it was hardly surprising that they got him down at times.

The twins grew friendly with Paul Day. A strong bond formed between them. Day's songs reflect increasingly the way in which their tormented inner feelings awoke a response in his own mind.

It was noticeable that Day resorted to sci-fi imagery to express the division he and the Howe twins experienced between themselves and 'ordinary' life. A fairly early song, 'Year By Year the Evil Gains', appropriates the title of an actual SF story: [1]

> *City against city, town against town,*
> *Song against silences,*
> *My body against my brains*
> *As the entropic suns sail down ⊷*
> *Year by year the evil gains.*

[1] 'Year By Year the Evil Gains' in *New Writings in SF 27*, edited by Kenneth Bulmer, 1976.

Later, sci-fi imagery helps express an attractive sense of distance, as in the immediately popular 'How's the Weather in Your World', which has now become something of a standard:

> *Our heads are together on the pillow —*
> *How's the weather in your world?*

The same year yielded 'In the Midst of Life', where the same sense of a tranquil alienation is conveyed:

> *And when you turn to me*
> *Silence falls into a green darkness*
> *And the light devours*
> *Cities, skies, your eyes.*

Less successful was 'On Tomorrow's Avenues', where the lyricism again conveys alienation, and the too-determinedly surrealist 'The Thunder of Daffodils Underfoot'. There is also 'Anyone's World', where the use of the unexpected number 'four' points to some actual experience; had the subject-matter of the lyrics been stolen out of psycho-analytic textbooks, as one critic unkindly suggested,[1] we should expect the number to be two or three or even seven:

> *In anyone's world   Four is the most*
> *Time's under glass   People are mirrors*

The idea that we can at best hope to experience no more than four people or character-types, however numerous our acquaintances, is interesting. But it may be that the lyric is talking more directly of a small world containing only Tom, Barry, Paul Day, and – who was the fourth member? No doubt the fourth member was Laura Ashworth. The ambiguity in this song may not be deliberate, but Day was soon employing such devices with intent. Even the driving song, 'Valley of the Chateau', conceals a pun (The Valley

[2] Colwyn Thomas, 'The Two Shots that were Heard Round the World', *Sunday Times*, 23 May 1982.

of the Shadow of Death) made the more sinister by its being
unstated – though pointed to by the rhyme-scheme.

> *Valley of the Chateau*
> *Valley of the Chateau*
> *Valley of the Sacred Chateau –*
> *Where none of us can take a breath*

The mood of the earlier songs is generally that of a child's
fairy story. Where there is a menace, the central character
is immune to it through his innocence. 'Two-Way Romeo'
is an obvious exception to this rule, but that song was com-
missioned and written before Day had met the Howe twins.
It is only a concoction. The recipe was mine.

We see Day being drawn gradually into a unique rela-
tionship with the twins and the girl, and learning to face it
through his lyrics. He finds it threatening, as in 'Valley of
the Chateau', and 'Probability A'. Sometimes its grotesquery
can be expressed as comedy, as in the 'Serenade from a
Cerise Satellite', with its repeated line

> *One girl   three loves   fifteen arms*

With the rocketing success of the Bang-Bang, the sexual
imagery of their songs became much more open, for instance
in 'Year of the Quiet Lips':

> *smiling without speaking*
> *perfect giving perfect taking*
> *healing, feeling, sealing, mutely appealing*
> *haven for all comers stealing*
> *quiet sips   my summer year is here*
> *year of the quiet lips*

Patently, it is no dumb girl being addressed. The driving
vigour that marked Day's performance on-stage becomes
linked in the lyrics with a new outspokenness. Although the
title 'Girl Outside the City' suggests isolation, both words
and music speak of confidence:

56

The girl outside the city
Let it all flow by
Let it all flow by
She's a part of me
The typhoon's eye
The typhoon's eye
The air in the airport
As we up and leave the city
For the places where the pulse beats stronger
Where the loving's madder   where the nights are longer
Where she's so much gladder
Let it all flow by
Let it all flow by

Even in the period of the true love-songs, a note of reproach often sounds. Or it does on paper. What Day wrote tenderly, was belted out with contradictory ferocity. The performance gives us their version of the complex love affair.

> *Oh you are all things to me*
> *Lover and vampire*
> *You keep three lovers happy*
> *A phoenix of their fire*
>
> *In this world I'm love's tourist*
> *Another head is dreaming of your beauty*
> *Our love is a forest*

(from 'Our Love is a Forest')

The line repeated in each verse, 'You keep three lovers happy', may seem like praise the first time; in repetition, it becomes more of a reproach. Even the freer moral code of our time has done nothing to extinguish jealousy.

The phraseology of the songs becomes more complex, the ideas move away from the traditional enclosed world of calf-love. No doubt it was Laura, with her more educated background and extensive reading, who influenced Day's vocabulary and the terms in which he celebrated her. This is most noticeable in the later songs, and in particular in the best song he ever wrote, his one song which mentions Laura by name, 'I was Never Deaf or Blind to her Music' (see Appendix), with such lovely lines as 'Time was, her alchemy was all upon me'.

This magical song, which one critic referred to as 'The Rhapsody in Blue of the Eighties', was included in the Bang-Bang's best record, 'Big Lover'. Here the Bang-Bang set aside what many regard as their natural coarseness, particularly in the three sci-fi tracks which are also included in the Appendix to this volume, 'Big Lover', 'Star-Time', and 'Bacterial Action'. These are by no means love-songs. But they show Day rejoicing in the new perspectives which Laura brought to his life, and the new power of expression he found for them.

After this peak, there seems to be a recession. The structure of the love affair was probably too unstable to last for long. 'The Vocabulary of Touch' has certain ingenuity, but the musical form reaches back to the conventions of the thirties for its closing lines:

> *Wetness and heat and a tired kiss*
> *All verbs expended*
> *Your breasts   your shoulders   your eyelids closing*
> *The sentence ended*

Trouble developed on the Scandinavian tour. The Bang-Bang came to blows with Paul Day on stage. And as soon as they arrived back in England, Laura disappeared. My belief is that her Church of England upbringing had instilled strong feelings of guilt in her and she could endure the *ménage à quatre* no longer.

On that unhappy tour, the Bang-Bang performed live, for the first and last time, 'Passport to Another Planet', which

I regard as Paul Day's farewell to Laura. A tired nostalgia is aimed at and achieved, despite ugly idiom in the first verse; in the last verse, isolation is again closing in on the singer.

> *You in your torn peace sleeping*
> *Come from a southern town*
> *Let me wake you with a cup of coffee*
> *Parting's going to bring us down*
>
> *Now with your passport to another planet*
> *You take your sex and sunlight away*
> *Life's going to be mere imitation*
> *Plastic lovers   cardboard day*
>
> *You dress that burning body*
> *And for the last time cling*
>
> *Already there's a glass case closing over*
> *The days when we had everything*

There was a glass cage closing over the age of the Bang-Bang. They were a phenomenon that came and went in under three years. The Howe twins were finished with the disappearance of Laura. Barry had some kind of emotional breakdown which I am convinced was nothing to do with over-use of the stun-gun. I engaged a special nurse to look after them at Humbleden, as well as persuading their elder sister, Roberta Howe, to be with them for some weeks. Paul Day patched up his quarrel with them and then announced to me that he was leaving to strike out on his own in the States.

The Bang-Bang's three-year contract with Bedderwick Walker expired; neither side sought to renew. It is always better to be a coward and live to fight another day. The life of novelty groups is always limited. The twins returned to

Norfolk and the obscurity from which they came. When all the charges of exploitation are made, I remain convinced that I was their benefactor. And the public heard a lot of good pop music.

Which is what I'm in business for.

CHAPTER 5

Continuation by Roberta Howe

These accounts have covered the period of my brothers'
lives during which they were world-famous. Much remains
to be said concerning the later period of their obscurity. I
am the one person with enough knowledge to fill in those
missing months.

It was terrible dealing with them at Humbleden. When I
arrived, poor Barry was exhausted enough to be bedridden,
much to the frustration of Tom, who found himself tethered
in one spot. I calmed him as best I could. He cried again,
as he had many times, for a surgeon to set him free from
his brother, although he knew that there was no operation
which could spare the lives of both him and his brother.

'Then set me free and let me live! I'm the normal one!'
cried Tom.

I soothed them as I so often had before. Paul Day, the
guitarist, a nice quiet boy, spent a lot of time with them,
mostly playing cards.

The day after Tom's outburst, Barry had a similar fit of
anger, calling his brother a murderer and betrayer and I
know not what else besides. They had a terrible fight, each
trying to tear apart from the other, and falling off the bed
in their struggles. Paul called for Nick Sidney, who applied
his gun to Barry's head. It was the first time I had seen this
done, but at least it brought peace.

'You'd better take us back home, Rob,' Tom said. 'We're
all finished up as far as any co-operation goes. All I want's
to be quiet and peaceful by the sea.'

When Barry came to, he seemed almost in a stupor. He
said nothing. He staggered over to their wash-basin and Tom
neither helped nor hindered, like he was pretending he

wasn't there. I looked on Barry washing himself as of old, when he and Tom were children, and I noticed how he still took care to wash the silent face beside his. Whereas he would never touch any part of his brother's body. (That I know, and state it here to settle certain rumours that have circulated; other lies I will also settle in due course.)

Next day, we left Humbleden. Funnily enough, when Nick and the others came out on the steps to wave us good-bye, both Tom and Barry wept. I went with them back to L'Estrange Head. I had pleaded with father to let us move to somewhere less deserted. He refused. The time now arrived for me to feel glad that he had done so, hoping that wild nature, with the proximity of open land and sea, would have a healing influence on my brothers. Unfortunately, that was not to be the case.

I was pleased that Paul Day accompanied us on the journey home. He proved Tom and Barry's best friend, after all that had happened to them and all they had done, yet he scarcely said a dozen words all journey. To think they were world-famous yet so isolated!

Paul would not come over to the Head with us, offering as an excuse that he had to be back in Humbleden that night. I drove him to the railway station at Deepdale Norton. I got out of the car with him while my brothers remained silent inside. Paul said good-bye to them quite formally, shaking both their hands.

Nobody was about. The station might have been closed. Before he turned to buy his ticket for the train, Paul spoke to me quite urgently, in a low voice.

He said, 'I hope they'll be up to scratch soon. Something marvellous has died . . . I don't know . . . I want to tell you that your brothers and me had a good friend in Laura. I won't make no bones about it, she was a lover to all of us, a real prize girl and absolutely unorthodox how she carried on. That's why they were all against her, Nick and all . . .

'What she did was fine, really fine, nobody knows, though

there are bastards about who tried all the time to finish it all. She's the best girl you could ever meet, a real life-giver, though she's gone now, more's the bloody pity. Oh, I'd have whitewashed the sky for her, believe me. Don't listen to any malice, we were the ones involved and we could tell you different if we was the kind to speak up, like those others.'

'I see. Paul, is there any chance I can get in touch with Laura if my brothers want to see her again?'

He looked down at the concrete steps and shuffled his feet.

'You ought to get her over if you can.'

'Have you any idea where she might be now?'

'She must be suffering, wherever she is. I only hope she can hold up. She always walked on a precipice. It was Chris Dervish, now dead, who did for her. He freaked her out on acid – maybe you've heard. Poor love, she tore all her clothes off of her. That lawyer guy Couling was down at Humbleden that week-end, and there was a gang-bang, with him involved and of course bloody Dervish, and most of the rest of the lads. Me too, yes, me too. She was so plastered. She was round the bend for a while after. I will say that I've never forgiven myself, and this time I have had my chance to make it up to her.'

'Did Mr Bedderwick get to know about this?'

'Couling went bananas after, paid us all to keep our traps shut. I really love Laura, Robbie, and would do anything for her, anything. It's not just guilt. She has a heart of gold, I mean I wrote all my best songs about her and that's about all I'm good for. I doubt if I shall ever write another song. I'm washed up. Maybe I can get myself together in the States.'

'Why did you all break up like this?'

He stared bitterly across the marshes.

'They was all against us. You can't imagine what the pressure's like. Success is a bastard. In the end she couldn't stand it. And Barry is cruel, full of rage against what he is.

You know, it's his make-up, I don't *blame* him in any way.'

'Barry's never cruel. It's just what he's suffered.'

Paul scratched his head and did not contradict. 'Oh, he loved her same road as Tom and me did. You had to love Laura . . . Well . . . Anyhow, I thought I'd tell you so as you can understand. Hope you don't mind the grisly details.'

'Where can I get in touch with Laura?'

He gave me a light kiss on the cheek.

'If I knew that, d'you think I'd be hanging round here?'

A man came out of the station and pointed at a board we had not noticed. A sign on it announced that there would be no more trains that day. There was a one-day strike involving the footplate men of the region.

Paul would not come back to the Head with us. In the end, we left him standing in the sunshine. It was the last we saw of him.

That year was the very hot summer. The drought became so severe that wildlife began dying. All the windows of our house were open for weeks on end. Our poor old retriever Hope got a stroke from the heat and died; we buried him in the dunes. My brothers used to swim in the sea and the dykes every day. They took to going naked again, as when they were boys, despite my father's complaints, for we had many visitors to the bird sanctuary as summer advanced. The curse of silence had fallen on them.

A day came when Laura Ashworth showed up. She came over in Bert Stebbings' tourist boat from the Staithe just as if she was a tourist. First thing I knew, there was this woman tapping at the kitchen door. It was still funny not having Hope to bark at visitors. I dried my hands and went to see who it was.

She looked ever so old and smart at first, so I couldn't grasp who she might be. I'd expected a teenager, I don't know why, instead of this lady in her thirties, in a skirt and everything. I must have appeared a proper fool in my fluster.

She wore a tasselled suede jacket with a white blouse under, and a suede skirt and sandals to match the jacket. Her hair was brown and blonde in streaks, and her face also brown and slender, with pleasing light hazel eyes. She was willowy, with a nice breast and legs – very attractive, I would say, once you got used to the shock. She was what I would call a lady, and self-possessed, as ladies are.

So I gave her a cup of tea and told her that Tom and Barry were away over the marsh somewhere. I asked where she had been since she disappeared but there was no straight answer to that. All she said was that she had changed her life-style but that she wanted to see Tom and Barry again.

To that I gave her no straight answer, but kept my trap shut. She tried some general conversation, remarking how bleak and flat L'Estrange Head was.

'Not when you get to know it, Miss Ashworth. There isn't a level space anywhere. We've got a lake and lots of little creeks, and in the more favoured spots elder and haw-thorn grow – not to mention wild roses and blackberries. It's a very pretty place for them as likes it.'

She then asked me direct if I wished her to see Tom and Barry.

'Are you sure you should see them, Miss Ashworth? I ask for your sake as much as theirs.'

Did they want to see her? she asked. Did I think she would be bad for them? Not in any attacking way, more like genuine questions.

I went into some rigmarole about how she had left them once and perhaps things ought to stay that way. I wanted her to interrupt but she listened very patiently, sitting on one of our old kitchen chairs, holding her mug of tea, and staring out at the ruin of the abbey beyond our window. Suddenly I saw that she was silently weeping. I was glad my father was over at the warden's hut.

'I've no wish to be unkind, Miss Ashworth, but if everyone is going to get upset all over again, then perhaps it's better . . . I mean, did you consider enough before you came here?'

She dried her eyes and apologized. She drank her tea. 'You see, I've nowhere else to go. This bloody age we live in, we're all outcasts and strangers – it isn't just your brothers, Miss Howe. All the old values have disappeared, been laughed out of court, and we've got nothing in their place.'

'Still, that's not a very good reason for coming to L'Estrange Head.'

At that she laughed. 'Oh, I daresay the rot's set in here, too.'

So I poured her some more tea, and I said to her straight, 'Miss Ashworth, I don't see what you have to be upset about. If you loved my brothers and they loved you, then life was better for them than ever it was before. And we know such things don't last, alas. If you feel bad about letting them both make love to you at the same time, you don't need to do so. I don't see that's a disgrace. Forgive me for speaking frankly with you.

'I told them years ago that if they ever had a girl it would have to be that way, they'd have to share. Else it would be unbearable for the one who was left out, isn't that so? I'm pleased that such a girl came along.'

'Good God!' she said. She stared at me, then reached out and clutched my hand. 'I'm so used to opposition that approval takes me aback . . .'

'Well, I do approve, if it's any of my business, and I don't think you have any need to complain. Many a girl would think it was the peak of delight to have two good young chaps at the same time.'

Well, then she sort of laughed, and we both laughed, and she looked at me askance. She said she'd go along the beach and see how Tom and Barry were.

At the back door, she paused and said, 'I suppose you think I'm here for more of the same thing?'

I smiled at her. You could not help it. 'Probably,' I said.

An odd thing about our Head was that everyone remarked on how flat it was; yet it was not at all. There were endless places to hide, as Bert Stebbings and I could tell you. So I didn't see Laura or my brothers again until the long dusk had fallen, when they appeared at the back door, staggering, both with lips and noses bleeding. No sign of Laura.

'You've been fighting again, you bloody fools,' cries my father, jumping up and flinging down his encyclopaedia. 'One of these days, you'll kill yourselves.'

'I'm putting up with him no longer,' cries Barry, making over to the draining-board, and seizing up the kitchen knife. Tom resists him, trying to trip him over. Both swear violently while they wrestle.

Barry makes as if to cut the two of them apart through the living flesh. They have nothing on, and sand falls from their sweating bodies as they abrade each other in the struggle. My father and I both jump up. I scream. My father, being powerful, finally manages to get the knife away from them. They both fall back against the sink, never able to get away from each other, the flesh that joins them stretched into bars.

When they have calmed down slightly, I ask where Laura is. It almost starts another fight.

Tom is in a kind of cold fury, his face very pale. 'I can say or do nothing with this madman at my throat,' says he. 'It is not possible to talk to her or touch her without his interference.'

'He tries to monopolize her,' cries Barry. 'So what do you expect? She's gone off on Bert's last boat to the mainland. I wish I were dead, I wish I were dead. Even more I wish this parasitic bastard were dead.'

The tendons and skin between them were contorted as

they held themselves as far apart as possible, Barry knocking his head against his sleeping one in his longing to tear himself away from his brother.

'Is she coming back?' I asked.

'Why should she?' cried Tom. 'Why should she, to be pestered and threatened by this bully.' He burst into angry tears. Always infuriated by such displays, my father shouted to him to stop.

As for me, I was greatly disappointed. I had hoped Laura would stay and help the boys be more normal. She would have been company for me. A feeling of desolation came over me, and I ordered them both up to bed.

Watching them fight their way upstairs, reflecting on their perpetual enmity and my father's general indifference, I wished that when they had left they had never come back. I wished Bert would marry me and take me away. I stood paralysed in the middle of the room, wishing myself a thousand miles off.

My father put the knife down, settled himself at the table and scanned the bird encyclopaedia again.

'It's botulism, that's what it is, Robbie,' he said, 'that's what's doing for the mallard.' He stroked the dead duck that lay by his hand.

'I wish it would do for all of us!' I rushed out and ran away over the dunes.

After Laura's visit, the last stage of my brothers' struggle began. When I returned to the house and crept up to my bed, I could hear them arguing and shouting in their room. The noise got so furious at one stage that I went out and paused before their door. Of course my father slept through it all, dreaming peacefully of the mallard dying in the summer marshes, no doubt.

My brothers were having a vulgar old row, details of which I had best not repeat. Tom wanted them to go off and find Laura. Barry said he was being greedy and refused to leave the Head; they could rape women visitors who came to see the birds. They brought in other charges against each other, unresolved quarrels from the past. They had fuel enough.

I was about to creep back to my room when they started another fight. In no time Barry was shouting, 'Come on, come on, I'll break your back for you, you gutless little git!' I heard the window swung wide, and a scuffle. I ran in – just in time to see the strange double-backed creature leap from the window.

Running to look out, I saw them pick themselves up from where they were sprawling. Punching, kicking, biting shoulders and jaws, they struggled away into the dark.

I called. They paid no heed. I returned to my bed.

Next day, that deadly antagonism was continued. They appeared mid-morning, fighting to eat and stop the other eating. They broke a chair and struck each other with bits of it. For the first time, I could not find it in my heart to be patient. They ran out, a mad animal fighting itself to death. After that, they did not intrude in the house again. They had become feral.

The heat wave continued, in perfect days and brazen nights. I swam last thing in Compton Water, when the visitors had left, relishing the calm last light in the western sky. Ducks continued to die, and not only ducks. My father doggedly piled up poisoned gulls, Canada geese, mute swans, snipe. Our little lagoons and ditches were sick, our lake choked; their waters had turned the colour of gherkins, thickened by algae. Dead fish, bream and the like, floated to the surface. Foul smells spread across the Head.

During the nights, I would wake, hearing my brothers scream and swear outside, sometimes near, sometimes far away. During the days, when the heat rose, I would occasionally see them running with that gait personal to them, across the dunes, in an endurance race of their own devising. I hardened my heart against them.

A conservation officer from the National Naturalists'

Trust came and examined our dying wildlife. The drought had properly upset the balance of nature. A strain of bacteria causing botulism had bred in decaying ooze in the exposed beds of ponds and ditches drying under the sun. Their poison was attacking the birds' nervous systems. Every day, deaths mounted. My father dug trenches among the dunes and buried the victims, grebes, gulls and ducks.

The heat, the atmosphere of death, and the disappearance of my brothers brought a suspension to life. Everything waited.

The only punctuation to our days was the arrival of two men from the NNT to help us save some of the affected wildlife. Father and I worked with the men, day after day, pulling a hand-trailer across the undulating grass and marram. We worked all the way to Great Aster, the marsh terminating the Head to the east. We visited Norton Lake, our one stretch of fresh water, which was replenished through dykes and wooden sluices from Deepdale Marsh, inland. The eight-acre lake looked beautiful, with purple loosestrife in bloom along its banks. But it was sick. Dead fish floated belly up. When we stirred the bed of the lake, it gave off a reek of hydrogen sulphide. We collected two black-headed gulls, a great-crested grebe, and a cormorant too ill to dive and escape us. Botulism Type C had attacked all these birds. The cormorant's neck was so weak that it could not lift its head. Some of these poor creatures would recover when moved to uncontaminated water elsewhere.

Sometimes, I looked up from our task and spied my brothers some way away. They were watching us. The whole landscape shimmered in the heat – it was difficult to believe they were there. As we worked along the southern fringes of our little domain, along by Little Ramsey, Great Ramsey, and the saltings, towards Overy Mussel Strand and Great Aster, I would look inland and see a silver thread of holiday traffic winding along the coast road. I realized how isolated we were.

Father hardly spoke from dawn to sunset. His heart was breaking to see his creatures die. Yet some creatures flourished in the drought. We saw grass snakes for the first time on the Head. Sand lizards scuttled everywhere – pretty little nervous creatures. Most unpleasant was a plague of ladybirds, which sprawled copulating in their millions all over the house, getting into beds and food and clothes, piles of them everywhere like fresh blood.

The sun baked my unfortunate brothers black. They were starving each other, taxing each other to death, wearing each other down, regardless of consequences. I feared that they devoured carcasses of poisoned birds. Visitors to the sanctuary were terrified by them. A London journalist on a weekend trip to Blakeney filed a story with his paper which appeared under the headline 'Minotaur in a Mallard Sanctuary'. We had a special boatload of tourists after that. My father drove them off by firing his sporting rifle over their heads. He was almost as strange as his sons.

Our little isolated world stank of death. I hung bunches of sea lavender and the pungent sea wormwood in the kitchen. I locked the doors at night. My brothers cried outside my window – blessings, pleas, obscenities. I could not bear it. I went away in Bert Stebbings' boat and stayed with my aunt at the Staithe. But I had no place there, and returned to the Head late the next day.

Bert took me back in his boat. It was nine in the evening as we chugged up The Run. L'Estrange Head was deserted of its daytime visitors. Its bare extent lay quiet under the last of the sun. I could see the abbey ruin and our house against it, with a light burning in the kitchen, where my father would be reading or stuffing a dead bird. Never before had I felt the desolation as hostile.

My brothers heard the chug of the boat's engine as we rounded into Cockle Bight. They came running like a four-legged beast into the shallows towards us, brandishing sticks in their outer fists, shouting, cursing me and Bert.

'They've gone proper barmy, Robbie, my love, that they have – I wouldn't trust yourself to them,' Bert said. He shouted out to them to control themselves.

They paused. They stared out across the darkening waters towards us. The Deeping Sands light started its quick flashing out to sea. For the first time in my life, I was scared of my own brothers. They were not my brothers any more. Instead, they were something – elemental is perhaps the word.

'Come back home with me, Robbie,' Bert said. He stopped his engine.

Those were the words I wanted to hear him say. Tom tried to wade out towards our boat. At once Barry lifted up his right, inner arm, and locked it behind Tom's head so as to thrust it forward. Of all the indignities they had inflicted on each other, this move was one, I felt sure, they had never managed before, because of the tightness of the ligaments binding them together.

Tom kicked out at Barry's legs and a fight started. They fell into the swelling sea, bellowing. They disappeared, though terrible thrashings marked where they were.

'Oh, quick, Bert!'

Without a word, Bert let in the clutch and we surged forward. He made a sweep round, cut the engine, threw out his little anchor, and jumped overboard, all in one practised series of movements. I jumped in after him. The water was up to the top of my thighs.

Bert got on top of my brothers and started pulling. Tom's head came up, water pouring from it, his mouth a wide hole gasping for air. Barry's head came up, and the third head. But Tom grabbed it by its hair and dragged them under again. Bert caught him round the throat and wrenched him above the surface.

Somehow we dragged them to the nearest bit of beach between us and dropped them there. Tom was still fighting and coughing and swearing but Barry was too exhausted even to do that. We worked at his lungs, but he merely

72

groaned. He was unconscious, his face livid. Suddenly it was dark and chill.

Glaring up at me with an alarmed expression, Bert said, 'He looks real bad. We'd best take them to Dr Collins' clinic in Norton.'

As he spoke, Barry groaned louder and went into convulsions, sitting up – still unconscious but his eyes staring – and bellowing for breath. His face was distorted, his neck thick. He flung Tom about in his agony.

'Quick, it's his heart!' cried Tom, clutching at his own heart.

Bert and I stood up. The sky was darkening overhead with night winding in across the marshes. Barry's noise was terrible – both his and that other face were black as they writhed in pain.

'It's a coronary attack,' I said. 'Oh, Bert! Better not to move them. I'll go and get Dad. You go back in the boat and get Dr Collins. Quick as you can. Tell Aunt. Look, ask Aunt to phone Henry Couling, that lawyer, will you? She has his number. We may need his help.'

'Don't leave us!' Tom cried.

I was suddenly all cold and practical. Without waiting to see Bert go off, I told Tom to lie as still as he could and went on the run across the dunes for father.

The rest of that night is best not told in detail. When Barry's attack was over, father and I got him with Tom's help back to the house. We tucked them up under blankets on the floor of the living room. It was best not to attempt the stairs. Barry was in a deep slumber, seemingly more dead than alive. Both his face and the other one were flushed. Tom also complained of pains, which was scarcely surprising, considering their connecting circulatory system. His breathing was fast and shallow; he was sweating a good deal and looking thoroughly frightened. When I bathed his head and shoulders, a crust of dirt came away.

Bert came with Dr Collins on the low tide at six the next

morning, when colour had newly returned to the world about us. It was impossible to make headway up The Run in a small boat against an incoming tide.

Everyone loved Dr Collins, mainly because she looked like sixteen years of age and had the stamina of a carthorse. She was a small neat woman with bobbed hair. She examined both of my brothers before giving them an injection which put them out. Her diagnosis was that Barry had suffered a thrombosis. It was imperative to get them to the hospital in Holt quickly.

Nobody argued with Dr Collins.

Father roused himself from his self-absorption for once and took charge of things. We shipped Tom and Barry over to the Staithe in Bert's boat, and Dr Collins phoned for an ambulance. Before the ambulance arrived at the Staithe, Barry had another violent attack. Both the boys were in a bad way. The terrible heat did not help matters.

On the way to the hospital, Barry had a further seizure, and died.

CHAPTER 6

Statement by Dr Alyson Collins

Roberta Howe has asked me to write a note about the Howe twins, and of course I am happy to do so. The Howe twins are as celebrated in the literature of teratology as are the Siamese twins. However, I intend this to be a personal record, not a medical paper.

The sibling hatred that existed between Tom and Barry was accentuated by their inseparability. In character they were totally different, both dominated by an impaired parent-relationship. This encouraged neurotic passivity in the case of Tom. Under ordinary circumstances, Tom would have signified submission in any rivalry situation by withdrawal; linked to his aggressive brother, he was unable to withdraw, and so was in a perpetual anxiety state, his self-assertive faculties constantly over-taxed. Which is not to imply that he was not often the aggressor; as psychotherapists understand, worms turn, and Tom in hysteria frequently attacked his dominant brother.

In most reminiscences of the Howe twins, Barry is generally cast as the villain. I am less certain of this. Admittedly he was aggressive, yet it is doubtful if he would have attracted attention had he been free to pursue his own course. There is some evidence of obsessional neurosis in his attempts to control Tom, but this is hardly to be wondered at, when we reflect how he was forever unable to act as a free agent capable of spontaneous action.

Anxiety quotients were high in both Tom and Barry. In childhood and after, they had been examined by experts at irregular intervals. After every examination, they suffered traumatic outbursts of activity, characterized by violence. This suggests masked fears about the severance – a traumatic event following which they would have to make their way through life alone, as individuals, unsupported in a world which had already graphically demonstrated the inadequacy of parental love.

Their meteoric rise to being pop superstars reinforced the underlying fears that either would have been useless on his own; while their sexual jealousy rendered continued propinquity intolerable. Resultant tensions destroyed them.

My understanding is that constant high anxiety quotients promoted serum cholesterol levels in the bloodstream which accelerated a narrowing of the arteries of the heart. The formation of blood clots was promoted, and so the coronary attacks occurred. Since the Howe twins had a communal circulatory system, it is a matter of accident that it was Barry rather than his twin who suffered from the thrombosis.

We were fortunate that Sir Allardyce Stevens, whose work on artificial hearts and pacemakers is well known, happened to be at Holt Hospital when the twins arrived. Sir Allardyce was attending a symposium, and had had occasion to examine the twins professionally during the period of their success as the Bang-Bang. He immediately took charge of the case.

At this juncture, Barry Howe was already dead. Which is to say, his heart pump had failed and was merely fibrillating in response to the linked pump of Tom's heart. Tom had responded to the shocks to his system with hysterical attacks. The male nurse with him in the ambulance, Mr V. S. Porter, had administered a sedative, and Tom was still unconscious when the double body was wheeled into Holt operating theatre.

Sir Allardyce's examination showed severe infarction of the right ventricle, with necrosis of cellular tissue there and in the adjoining superior vena cava. The layman must understand that this examination entailed open-heart surgery in which cardiac catheterization was employed. In other words, the preliminary steps towards a heart transplant were already taken before Sir Allardyce decided that a heart transplant was necessary. I explain this because criticism of that decision has circulated, mainly thanks to an ill-informed lay press. The decision represented a small step on, and an inevitable one if the Howe twins were to survive. No competent surgeon in Sir Allardyce's position would have decided otherwise.

An APPCOR (Auto-Powered Prosthetic Cardiac Organ Replacement) of the correct specification was to hand. It was installed in place of the defective organ, and the installation proceeded without a hitch.

I was moved by my first sight of the Howe twins. They were both handsome young men. It was an ill turn of fate that they had not entirely separated in the womb. Given this conjoined condition, they should not have been encouraged to survive post-natally. Such is my professional opinion. I am aware of certain moral considerations. I am also aware that medical men have a natural streak of curiosity; given all the wonderful modern adjuncts of their profession they are sometimes tempted to prolong life in order to see what will happen, without regard to the grief incurred by the survivors. In this respect they are little better than Victor Frankenstein, bringing a creature to life without any thought of what might follow.

Now Sir Allardyce was patching one such example of regardlessness with another of the same kind. He was a brilliant surgeon who had a brilliant opportunity come his way; it was hardly to be expected that he would not take it.

I travelled with the twins in the ambulance from Deeping Staithe to Holt, and was present during the 'death' of Barry. My own panel, my own patients, awaited me back in Deepdale Norton. I returned there as soon as possible, since I was unable to make myself useful at the hospital. However, such was my interest in the case, that I drove back to Holt when evening surgery was over. Sister Carrisbroke showed me to the ICU – and there were the Howe twins, with Tom propped up on a pillow and taking soup.

Barry lay back beside him against the banked mattress. His eyes were closed. His complexion was pale and blotched in comparison with the healthier colour of Tom's face. The other head lay silently against Barry's, in its usual position. Barry's breathing was normal. Tom was cheerful. As so often in APPCOR cases, the recovery-rate is impressive. When I drove back again to Norton, I gave Roberta Howe a lift from the hospital. She spent the night at her aunt's in Deepdale Staithe. She was tired but cheerful.

'I never seen Tom look so relaxed and content,' she said.

It was not for me to spoil her happiness by reminding her that the everlasting sibling struggle would resume as soon as Barry regained consciousness. At her Aunt's, a message awaited her from Mr Couling, the lawyer of the show business agency which had employed the Howe twins as singers, saying that financial support would be forthcoming from the agency. So I left Roberta in a state of subdued relief.

For the next few days, the media were full of accounts of the APPCOR operation, and photographs of the Bang-Bang were in circulation again. Then Sister Carrisbroke phoned me while I was taking evening surgery. She had alarming news. Barry had not recovered consciousness. Barry remained dead, despite his new heart.

On several occasions, the expanding frontiers of medicine have caused us to alter our conceptions of dying. Ever since the sixties of this century, it has become increasingly difficult to define the critical point at which life can be said to slip irretrievably into death. The Jacobean poet was near to the truth when he said that 'Death hath ten thousand several doors for men to take their exits'.

After surgery, I got in my car and drove the nineteen

miles to Holt. Doctors rarely think about death; on that journey, I had to force myself not to.

Sister Carrisbroke's professional manner was reassuring.

Brain cells undergo rapid amortization once their supply of oxygen is cut off. Thirty minutes after oxygenation ceases, irreversible deterioration commences. For some hours following Barry's thrombosis at Cockle Bight, Tom's heart had had to bear a double load for both bodies to survive. In terms of actual work, it had to pump one hundred and sixty gallons of blood an hour, and to keep that heavy fluid moving through the equivalent of 120,000 miles of veins, arteries, and capillaries. It failed to provide circulation enough for Barry's brain – to be precise, the vital neocortex, the essentially human sectors of the cerebral hemispheres.

Barry lived physically because of the APPCOR. Psychically, Barry was dead.

The APPCOR functioned perfectly. It would not restore the defunct brain tissue in the middle skull of those three tormented Howe skulls. Tom was now coupled to an animated corpse.

'And the . . . third head?' I asked the Sister.

She looked askance at me. 'The EEG shows a speeding-up of cortical and sub-cortical activity of low voltage in the third head.'

'What does that imply? It's waking up?'

She said, 'Barry's head is electrically dead. The third head appears to be moving towards a working state.'

'My God, what does Sir Allardyce say to that?'

'He's back in London, but keeping in touch.'

'I should damned well hope he is. Tom?'

'Since Tom knows nothing about *that*, he is pretty happy.' She laughed with an edgy note. 'He thinks he's got the place to himself. He's won his battle to be alone.'

Three weeks later, the twins, only one of whom was alive

according to classical definition, were permitted to leave hospital. Their devoted sister, Roberta, met them at Holt and took them back across The Run to L'Estrange Head.

The last act of the affair was played out there, and we have only Roberta's record of what occurred.

CHAPTER 7

Conclusion by Roberta Howe

It was hard to think of them as just Tom. After all, Barry was still *there*, his body working perfectly, thanks to the machine heart, the APPCOR. There was a difference, though, and in the main a difference we all enjoyed. Barry did not fight any more. He was meek and submissive – or his body was, I should say. This was such paradise for Tom that he was content to sit all day, in the house out of the heat, and generally in his bedroom, where he could stare across the ruins to the sea.

Dr Collins came over in Bert's boat to see how we were getting on. There was nothing to report but calm. Barry was gone – I can't say dead, because that never made sense to me, with his body walking round, whatever was technically correct. His head now lolled forward and his neck was lax, like the birds attacked by Botulism Type C. It often lay peacefully against the third head. To strangers, Tom and his double-body would have presented a strange sight.

Pleased though I was to have peace, the situation worried me – that I will not deny. The day after they were back on the Head, I went over to the Staithe to see Aunt Hetty and shop. Owing to the tourist trade, Mr Bowes at the stores had many more goods than in the winter, when there were only us locals to cater for. He had a rack of paperback books going cheap, among which I spied one entitled 'The Brain Simply Explained'. I bought it and took it back home to read.

Simply explained or not, much of the book I could not understand. One passage, however, stuck in my mind.

An arterial system delivers the oxygen to 10,000 mil-

*lion neurons. Similar intricate systems go to compose the
enormous complexity of the brain. Small wonder if
occasionally a connection malfunctions, as in a television
set. It co-ordinates and regulates the muscular systems of
the body, preserves a lifetime of human experience, and
functions as the centre of human awareness. The paradox
is that there are still sectors of the brain whose function we do not understand and, consequently, there may
be types of awareness of which we are still unaware.*

That was in Chapter One. 'Small wonder if occasionally
a connection malfunctions'! That must have been what
happened to poor Barry. Something had gone wrong in
their bodies at birth – it was reasonable to assume something had gone wrong in their brains.

I thought about the strange happenings that occur in our
brains, and wondered how the whole business could have
come about, while father and I worked the foreshore during that long afternoon, looking for sick birds. And that night
Tom had the first of his three dreams.

Well, I put it like that. Later, I recollected that during
the previous night – the first night he was back with us from
the hospital – Tom had cried out in the small hours; I had
heard his cry, then fallen back to sleep.

This time, it was about three o'clock when he began to
scream. It was a choking noise which gradually became
louder. I had never heard anything like it before. I was out
of my bed and running to him almost before I had come to
my senses. I darted past my father's room and into Tom's.

It was stifling hot in his room. The window was open, but
there was not a stir of breeze. The September moon was
two days off full, and its light poured in. Outside, beyond
the dunes, glittered the sea. As I ran to the bed I saw that
Barry's arm was across Tom's throat. It was withdrawn as I
entered, slithering quickly under the sheet.

I soothed Tom's forehead and comforted him until he
roused properly. He broke into long deep sobs which con-

82

vulsed his body. I sat there, muttering words of love to him, feeling so glad to be of some little help. All this while, Barry's face lay close on the pillow. It was that of a man sound asleep – expressionless but hardly what I would dare call dead, whatever the medicos said.

As Tom calmed down, I noticed that the eyes of the other head were slightly open. There was a glitter as of liquid under the heavy lids. Venturing greatly, I reached out and put my right hand over the eyeballs. I felt a distinct tremor beneath my fingertips.

At that I took fright. Giving a yell, I ran out of the room, back to my own. Standing by my bed, trembling, I heard Tom call me.

I went to the door, peering into the dark of the landing.

'Tom? You all right?'

'Please come and see me, Robbie. I had an awful dream.'

Of course, I mastered my courage and returned to him. He had propped himself up a bit, and the other two heads lay against each other like two bowls, half-hidden by sheet.

I held his hand. We just sat and looked at each other in the cool moonlight. His face glittered with sweat.

A curious impression settled on my mind: that this was my dream, that I was still in my bed. Both the noises and the silence, the light and the dark, seemed to me in that instant – I believe it was just an instant – to be more like something that goes on in a sleeping head than in reality.

Then Tom said, 'I've got to tell you my dream,' and the impression dispersed.

I suggested that we went down and had a cup of tea in the kitchen. As he pulled on his jeans, I saw that the Barry body was already wearing its pair; Tom had not bothered to undress it. The double body came down the stairs after me. Switching on the reading lamp downstairs, I looked fearfully at the third head, but it gave no sign of intelligence.

While we drank our mugs of tea, Tom related his dream, with a few comments here and there from me.

'They gave me sedatives every night in hospital . . . To-night was different. Open the back door and let some breeze in, Robbie! There's nobody out there to harm us . . .

'Well, my dream. It was so macabre, so connected. Not like a real ordinary dream . . .

'I was in a forest and rain was falling. A heavy, slow rain. It must have been falling for a long while. The forest floor was flooded. A steady stream pulled against my feet, making progress difficult.

'I could not see my way ahead. As I staggered onward, I kept buffeting myself against the trunks of the trees. They grew so close that my shoulders were bruised with repeated knocks. The journey had been so long. All the branches of the trees, high above my head, had intertwined. Darkness ruled in the forest. And yet – you know how these para-doxes occur in dreams – everything seemed bright, as if lit by an inward light.

'By another paradox which seemed natural at the time, I was not myself but a horse, or some other four-footed ani-mal. I'm not sure what. Perhaps a donkey – a pack-animal – because I was loaded down and consequently clumsy. And I was trying to get away from someone I hated. That urgency propelled me through the loathsome forest. The someone I wanted to get away from was helping me escape. He rode upon my back in a great raised saddle, draped with rugs and strings of jewels. With a black whip, he lashed me on.

'Blood burst from me. It fell like rubies, each large gobbet solid, gleaming, clattering to the ground. Yes, clattering to the ground, to dry stony ground.

'Where that ground was in relation to the rest of me, I can't tell, for I seemed to be still in the flood, and my difficulties increasing. When I glanced down, I saw that the flood-water had receded, leaving a carpet of thick mud. I saw that I was planting my hooves in the open mouths of great toads. No matter how I tried to avoid them, my hooves plunged into their open mouths, nailing them by their throats to the ground.

'My distress was so great that I began to cry in my sleep. I rolled, yet I could not roll over, for now another great lumbering beast was beside me. It was more like a giant sort of maggot or mummy – something corpse-like. Despite that, it was as if we were both galloping forward at a great pace. I could not out-distance the mummy. It was being ridden by a chimpanzee.

'Describing it like this, the dream sounds like a silly collection of wonders. It was all one situation – immediately understood, going on for ever. Suppose there is a life after death – if we were called on to describe our lives, we might be forced back on similar recital. I mean, we might not be able to describe it except as a list of its events. Like a fisherman who sees a river just in terms of its fish. Yet my dream was about the river – it wasn't about any of the events I've described at all, but about something else entirely. No. I'm telling it wrong.'

Tom gulped down some tea, then started again.

'I was aware that, whatever I was doing, I was actually doing something else. Oh, I know it sounds confused, but sometimes in dreams a state of confusion comes over as marvellous clarity.'

'Perhaps you were only half-asleep,' I suggested.

'Perhaps we are never more than half-awake . . . Anyhow, it now seemed as if I was no longer the horse, and had never been one. I was being carried on the back of one. It was a beautiful milk-white mare, and its rocking movement through the forest was sweet to me. But I still had to carry the great swaddled maggot with me. The trees were still flashing by, and it was dangerous to remain among them. Their trunks, I saw, were carved with elaborate carvings.

'Now the trees became more widely spaced. I gained courage. As we broke free of them altogether, I raised up the great maggot, lifted it above my head, and cast it away.

85

'Until the very second of parting with it, I had no interest in its nature. As I threw it, I became overwhelmingly curious as to what it was. Have you ever had the experience of being with a friend and finding nothing whatsoever to say to him; and then, as soon as he was gone, you think of a dozen important things you wanted to say? I met an old man when we were on tour in the North who told me he had married a girl he was madly in love with. Their marriage went all wrong right from the start. He hated her, he wanted to kill her because she disappointed all his hopes and broke his heart, and they got divorced. And immediately, he said, immediately he was free again, all the hate fell away, and he just longed for the girl, loved her more even than before, and could never look at another girl.

'A similar abrupt change of feeling came over me as I threw the maggot, or whatever it was, away from me. The bundle opened as it fell and I saw a small child's – a baby's – face looking up at me, rosy-cheeked, smiling, and absolutely innocent of any expectation of disaster. Then it hit the mud and at once sank into it, still smiling and trusting. To the last moment when its face was sucked under, it smiled up at me uncloudedly.

'Again there was division of feeling. Part of me rode on, haughty and glad to be free. Another part was overcome by grief. Great sobs rose up in me and cascaded from my mouth and nose and eyes. They fell in the form of diamonds, which rained to the ground and clattered there as previously my blood had done. My own noise woke me.'

He sat there for a while, head between his hands, so that three bowed heads confronted me.

'It was as if all that was good and valuable in my body was going from me,' he said. I clutched his hand, and we sat there in silence. Slowly the ashen light of dawn seeped in.

When Bert brought the first lot of tourists and birdwatchers to Cockle Bight, I was there waiting for him. He ferried me over to the mainland, where I borrowed his bike and cycled over to Dr Collins' surgery in Deepdale Norton.

She took me through into her office and made us both a cup of coffee as I poured out my tale of woe. I even brought myself to tell how the third head had opened its eyes.

'You mustn't be frightened,' she said. 'It's nothing – supernatural.' But she flicked her gaze away from mine, as if she was also alarmed.

'If Barry really is dead, if it's just the APPCOR that keeps his body – well, from putrefying ... then couldn't your surgeon do the operation and cut Tom free?' I asked. In the silence, I added, 'I know it would be a major operation.'

'I'm sure the possibility has occurred to Sir Allardyce,' Dr Collins said. 'Look, I'll phone him. I've got the number of his rooms in Harley Street; sit down, Robbie.'

Sir Allardyce was away. He was expected to look in to collect messages at 12.30. Then he was off to attend a one-day conference in Milan. His secretary promised that he would phone back at 12.30.

So I killed time. I went to see my Aunt Hetty, I had a drink and a sandwich in the pub with Bert and, at 12.20, I was back at the surgery. The call came through at 12.50.

Sir Allardyce had already been giving the matter consideration and was in consultation with his colleagues. I was to be reassured that the matter was still very much on his mind.

This much I heard, watching Sir Allardyce's talking head on the vision plate, before I interrupted. I told him that it was urgent, and that Tom was heading towards a breakdown, dragging a corpse round with him, and that I feared evil things unless help for him was forthcoming.

'I know exactly how you must feel, Miss Howe,' he said. 'But this is an absolutely unique case, and we must proceed with due care. We discharged your brother from hospital because he was unhappy there, but in my opinion it would be best if we brought him into a London hospital for observation.'

That sounded sensible to me. I said I would accompany Tom wherever he went.

Sir Allardyce looked at a calendar I could not see. 'Today is Wednesday. I shall be back in England on Friday. I will have my secretary arrange to have your brother collected in an ambulance on Friday and brought direct to London. Will that suit you? We will ring back and settle all the details of the arrangements with Dr Collins.'

So it was left. Only two more nights, then Tom would be in proper hands. I returned to the Head with relief.

Tom was restless that afternoon. He went out and wandered in the direction of the lake, returning not long before sunset. After exchanging a word with me, he slipped upstairs and played his guitar for half an hour. 'Two-Way Romeo' was one of the numbers. Then silence.

I cooked him some sausages and chips and he went to bed early. Father was stuffing a dead tern. I went out for a walk in the moonlight, strolling along what we always called The Feather, a fine curve of sand sculptured by wind, with water on either side of it. The night seemed limitless. I longed – oh, I don't know for what!

Father had retired when I returned. I crept softly upstairs, pausing outside Tom's room. Silence. I went to bed and slept eventually.

When I woke, I found myself sitting up. Clouds had blown over the moon and it was dark. Outside was the endless sound of the sea, inside, the noise of father snoring. Nothing else.

Getting up, I padded barefoot down the passage. Something compelled me to enter Tom's room.

The dimness fluctuated as clouds moved away from the moon's face. I saw three heads lying on the pillow. All were still. I approached. Tom's eyes were closed. Barry's eyes were closed. The eyes in the other head opened. Slowly, it turned towards me. The eyes opened wider.

As if this muscular exertion was a severe strain, the mouth fell open. Never to my knowledge had it opened before. I wondered if it contained teeth, but in the dull light only a black cavity could be seen. The eyes glittered. The general effect was one of imbecility. We stared at each other.

The noise of my own heart thudding made me move. Slowly, never letting my eyes leave the glittering ones, I edged towards Tom's side of the bed. The other head moved, keeping me always in sight. My outstretched hand reached Tom's shoulder, and I shook him, calling his name softly.

He muttered and stirred, but I could not rouse him. I shouted louder. Now a noise came from the black open mouth – a kind of a laugh, grating, dry.

'Tom!' I yelled. I slapped his face. He had a mug by his bed, half full of water. I dashed it in his face. At last he sat up.

'It's all sand,' he said.

'Oh, Tom, what's happening?' I cradled his head in my arms, and at last he was himself again.

'The other head's alive, Tom, it's coming alive.' We looked at it, but the eyes were closed again, the neck limp, in its usual position.

'I was dreaming about it.'

'What's its name, Tom, what's its name?'

'It hasn't got a name,' he said impatiently. 'It's dead, same as Barry.'

He climbed out of bed. Again I saw how perfectly co-ordinated were the movements of the other body, which Tom now controlled. But I felt something monstrous about him.

He went downstairs. There was nothing for it but to follow. He was splashing his face under the tap.

'Tom? Let's go and have a swim.'

'I was dreaming that I heard music. Perhaps it was your voice far off. It was a totally different kind of dream from yesterday's. It was more coherent – much more like a movie in some ways. But it was very malicious.

'And it went on for a long while.

'I dreamed I was a sort of tame creature or perhaps a person on a beautiful island – a small island much like an unspoilt England, with thickets and glades and lovely little intimate dells to be in. The only other people on the island were my master, who was some kind of alchemist – he wore rich gowns and a crown, which sounds silly but it was splendid in the dream – and his daughter, who was about my age and whom I loved dearly. She had long golden hair and a laughing mouth, and I remember seeing her dance by the edge of the waves. I dived in and out of the waves like a dog.

'All sorts of things happened, magical things, and they were all fun. I was tremendously happy. I could do magical acts as well, charm birds out of trees, whistle fish out of water, fly with the golden-haired girl over hills and the thatched roofs of villages, capture the sunrise.

'One day, I found a secret valley with a waterfall at the far end. It seemed to me the most delightful place, and I flung myself into the water. I think she was there too, and we were climbing up and up the cascade, laughing, when the alchemist caught me.

'He was furiously angry. Nothing I said made any difference to his fury. He had me trapped and I was dragged, as if by wolves, to a dark part of the island. I had never been there before. I realized that I was not a grand person. Seeing myself through the eyes of the alchemist, I realized that I was just a kind of rough animal, a sport. All the time that I was being dragged over broken ground, I was trying to shout and explain that I really was what I thought I was, not what he thought I was.

'The terror wasn't from the journey so much as from

this conflict of viewpoints. Because, in the dream, I could understand his conception of me to some extent, yet he could not understand mine, although mine was the truer one. Mine went deeper. Mine saw me from inside. Yet his view triumphed, simply because he was stronger – remorselessly strong.

'He took me to a great leafless tree. It must have been an oak. I saw its branches spread all over the sky like cracks in heaven. It was freshly split down the middle, so that its insides were open and all pale and yellow and glistening, like a disembowelled rabbit. Splinters hung all round the split, like the jaws of an animal with ferocious teeth. It opened still wider when the alchemist spoke. His voice was like thunder. I was crying for mercy.'

Tom paused and wiped his face.

'Telling you all this, I see it begin to sound like a dream about fear of punishment after sexual intercourse. But it wasn't half as simple as that in the actual dream. Because this wizard owned me, and there was a sort of counterpoint in the dream about how in fact he was quite powerless or rather he could invent nothing good, which was why I was malformed; whereas I had invented all the delights of the island. It's difficult to explain in words. When he grabbed me up, he rolled up all the good things as well, just as if they were the pattern on a Persian carpet. Carpet and I, we were thrown into the gaping entrails of the oak. Whereupon the alchemist slammed the tree shut and locked it with a great golden key.

'Immediately, it was like I had been transmuted into another person. I was just walking down a road in a rather boring way. I wasn't on the island any more. I had the carpet and I had the girl. She walked with me, much diminished. She had been writing a diary but now had hidden it and would not even tell me where it was; I did not wish to know where it was, but her silly refusal to speak about it chafed my spirit – I wanted free communion between us.

91

'Because of this, I led the way into a small village in a snug river valley, where we were surrounded by singing people all having great fun. Somehow I despised them. I was apart from them, though I sang with them. Yes, and I can even remember the song I sang . . .

'No, I have forgotten the tune, but I remember what the song was about. It was about a planet entirely covered by water. Over the ages the water became conscious. It flew away to another solar system, leaving a great world of sand where the tide had gone out for ever. I ran laughing over the golden sand, tremendously happy because again I was free. Things were hatching out of the dark damp sand, growing, spinning. They evolved into enormous complex castles and people and – oh, unimaginable shapes. It was wonderful.

'These inventions of my song invaded the snug river valley. Nobody paid any attention to them. Everyone left me. There was just the sand. Someone was standing by me, explaining. I did not like what he was saying, particularly as I could not see him.

' "Now you understand how the ocean became intelligent and developed life," he was saying, going into some long obscure scientific explanation.

'As he was speaking, I saw he was referring to a head which was growing out of the sand. It was more or less like a human head, but at the same time I could see inside it. It was all divided into different sandy floors and rooms, rather in the manner of a complex dolls' house. From it were pouring sandy thoughts. The thoughts were so powerful that I felt that they were overcoming me, and soon – I cannot tell you what terror I still experience when I say it – *the whole universe was becoming nothing but dry sand thoughts.* I saw that the stars shining overhead were just gobbets of sand.

'I was full of disgust. Even the sunlight was composed of fine particles of sand which threatened to suffocate me. With an effort, I began running for safety. The sand-grains stung my cheek. Even running was painful. Behind me, the head was growing bigger and bigger; it was virtually a planet in its own right.

'Looking down, I saw my limbs, my body, were composed of sand too. They began to crack and break . . . I scarcely dared wake up in case the dream proved to be real.'

We sat unmoving. At last I asked Tom if he would like a swim, just to convince himself that he was perfectly well.

'Just let me be. I'll sit here a while and recover. You go to bed, Rob.'

I pointed at the other head.

'That thing was awake, Tom. It is alive, it has thoughts. I don't think it is any friend of mine or yours. Suppose it wakes up fully and you're reduced to unconsciousness . . '

Tom stood up. I saw anger on his face. 'You get up to bed, girl, and don't talk nonsense. Leave me alone. I've been meddled with all my life.'

'But what do you think, Tom? Aren't you afraid? Why not talk about it?'

'There's nothing to talk about. Leave me alone.'

His manner had changed so abruptly that I was scared. I made my way reluctantly upstairs. My father was still snoring securely; it would have taken the Last Trump to wake him.

Well, I thought, one more night to go before we get Tom to proper care.

In the morning, he was gone. Father wanted me to do various odd jobs, and it was afternoon before I could strike out across the Head and find him. He was sitting dejectedly under the shade of an elder tree.

He seemed to be his old self again, saying he was sorry for his angry outburst. I coaxed him back home and gave him something to eat.

As the day wore on, he was increasingly listless. I kept looking at him when he was looking away. Barry's head was sunk down useless on to his chest. His cheeks looked gaunt and withered. The other head – was it not tense, as if feigning sleep? Hadn't its face filled out? Wasn't its hair less grey, less dead-looking?

Nameless fears filled me; I thought, if only we can get through the night, tomorrow the ambulance, London, proper care . . . I had not dared tell Tom yet what was planned. In a good mood, he would do as I bid. And he would surely want to be a separate person on his own if that was possible.

Towards dusk, I persuaded him to come and swim with me. Father sat at his table, watching us go, smiling vaguely.

The visitors had left. One or two solitary lights dotted the distance. The sea was flat, its surface heaving as if in a stupor. Not a wave broke. A leaden mist moved slowly over the sea like oil, the token of another day's heat already in preparation.

I stripped off my clothes and flung myself in the water. Tom waded in. As he launched himself, the other heads came up, and Barry's limbs went through swimming motions just as if he were alive. Just their two outer arms moved, the way of swimming they had adopted long ago. We did not stay in the water for long.

Above us in the sky shone the full moon, the Norfolk harvest moon.

'I think I'll sleep better tonight,' Tom said. 'I wish Laura was here.'

So we went to our bedrooms. Despite all my anxieties, I was soon fast asleep.

No sooner had my eyes closed – so it seemed – than the screaming started. It sounded like the snarling of a pair of wild dogs fighting. I staggered up, full of sleep, and again made my way to Tom's room, like a somnambulist. Again I had a strong impression that I was dreaming. Everything was precise in detail yet faint over-all, like a dream.

I went down the corridor like a swimmer, very slowly. When I entered Tom's room, the snarling had stopped. He was propped up in bed, smiling at me. He had arranged the sheet over the other heads.

It was so light in the room with the moonlight that his teeth gleamed when he yawned.

'What's happened? What was all that noise.'

'I had another dream.' That was all he said. He yawned again.

'Tom, are you all right?'

'It wasn't anything at first. I can't remember ever having the same feeling in a dream, or in real life. I was just nothing. Surrounded by nothing, I can't describe it. I had been sucked dry of all life, although I wasn't dead.' There he paused. When I thought he was going to say nothing more, he began again, in a dull voice.

'There just seemed to be wind about, blowing hither and yon. What slowly appeared was like part of my thoughts, at least at first. I was surrounded by desert. Only gradually did I realize that there were soldiers marching through it, whole ranks of them. Only they weren't soldiers; they were knights in armour. They trailed on through the sand with automatic tread.

'As I followed them, the revelation came that they were robots, things of metal, without consciousness. They were governed by a great distant machine, a vast metallic bowl like a flat face, like a huge radio telescope, which stood on the distant horizon.

'We marched and marched. There was a typical dream contradiction, because the lifeless robots occasionally fell and died and decayed as they hit the sand, so that we found ourselves marching over skeletons.

'Another contradiction – though it was all negative, nothing, it also seemed vastly important.

'The desert sloped down towards sunset and night. All the robots were marching into night, going from sun to dark and disappearing. It looked frightening. I didn't want to go that way. As I tried to leave them and go another way, I discovered that I had been turned into a robot too. I had no control over myself. I was forced to march into that destructive cloak of night.

'The night was artificially generated by the distant machine. I knew something about that machine but was unable to remember what. Now I was entering the dark, crying in despair.

'A powerfully-built man stood at the entrance, flogging everyone in.'

Tom paused, yawning again. Frightening though his dream sounded, he was telling it in mild tones, as if he were bored. I stood at the foot of the bed, listening, not moving.

'My emotion was so strong that there was a sort of break in the dream, almost as though I was being given time to dissolve. I felt that I was sinking to the bottom of an ocean – or rather, to the bottom of a multi-layered city which was drowned in an ocean. I could see lights, and people laughing and talking inside open windows as I floated down.

'As that awful downward drifting continued, I got to know more about the people. There were myriads of them, myriads and myriads, and they were all working on one immense project. The project was secret and involved building a super-weapon which would obliterate life on Earth – or wherever I was. The scheme went forward under immense secrecy, which was why the city had been built at the bottom of the ocean.

'Learning this information filled me with a sense of doom. I know the whole dream is filled with doom, but it was sharpened by the obsessive secrecy with which everyone worked. They were doing such a diversity of things towards the one end – pickling vegetables and embroidering cloth as well as working on all kinds of machines; apparently everything that was done in the city contributed to the one hideous end.

'What made it worse was that everyone was enjoying

96

themselves in a quiet way, despite the oppressive conditions and the secrecy. As I passed along the submerged street many a person I saw giving a crafty laugh or a sly snigger.

'It began to seem funny to me, too, although I knew it would all end in a mighty explosion . . .'

Again Tom paused. He snuggled down comfortably against his pillow. I waited for him to continue, but time lengthened and he said no more.

'Tom?'

He was asleep again. His breathing was even and regular.

I felt as unreal as a ghost, standing there at the foot of the bed. Drawn by an unknown compulsion, I moved round to where Barry's body lay covered. Grasping the corner of the sheet, I moved it: then, with an effort, pulled it down.

Barry's head lolled uselessly. But the other . . . Its eyes were regarding me. They glittered from under heavy lids, like oil. The mouth was partly open.

I brought myself to speak. 'Who are you?'

No reply. But it moved, craning up on its neck to regard me better. I took a pace back and repeated my question.

Then words formed in its mouth. 'You are part of my dream . . .'

The voice was suffocated, as if it came from under a pile of mouldy pillows.

'You aren't Barry. Who are you?'

Again a long wait, during which we stared at each other. Then it said 'My name is . . .' The word it spoke was instantly lost. I could not remember it as it was spoken and have been unable to since. 'I have been penned in this tree all my days.'

'You are not in a tree. You must be dreaming. Go back to sleep.'

The sense of effort when it spoke. 'Now I am escaping from the entrails of the tree. The two wicked ones who imprisoned me will be punished . . .'

Then silence. Then, with little regard for what it had just said, 'One has already died, one remains.'

On me was the strong spell of a dream from which I was unable to break free. 'You're wrong, you're wrong,' I was repeating, but it took no notice.

'I'll wake Tom,' I said.

Immediately, it was in action. Barry's body leaped up at me. Its arm came out and I was seized viciously by the wrist. The move was totally unexpected. It pulled me down to it, getting its other hand behind my neck.

I saw myself about to be dragged down on it, to have my face in contact with that face. At last I managed to scream. What a joy to make that noise, as when I first gave cry!

Tom's eyes opened.

He was immediately aware of what had happened. He twisted his body and struck the other's arm. The other released me and tried to grasp Tom by the throat. In its anger, it looked much like Barry, whose head lolled peacefully between the struggling pair.

A fearful battle took place between the two of them. I rolled off the bed and ran in fright to waken father. I burst into his room and beat him on the shoulder. Swearing, he came to his senses at last and climbed out of bed, grasping his sporting rifle which stood propped against the chair by his bedside. I had heard a rumpus on the stairs. When we got out there, the pair were down below. Father rushed down in the dark, shouting, I followed. Sounds of crashing and the back door bursting open.

The table in the living-room had been overturned. Father and I ran to the open door. It was almost as light as day outside. The twin figures were distant, still struggling together but making away across the low dunes. Father raised his rifle to fire, but I seized it and dragged it down, screaming at him.

'Are you mad, are you dreaming? That's your son out there!'

'They should never have been born.'

He stood where he was, wiping his mouth over and over again with the back of his hand. The struggling figures disappeared into the night.

Switching on the light, I looked at our old clock ticking on the mantelpiece. I saw with horror that it was only just a quarter to one in the morning. I wanted Bert to help me, and Dr Collins – anyone – but there was nothing we could do till daybreak.

Sleep overcame me. I dozed off in the old chair. When I woke, dawn was moving in across the flat prospects outside. I was stiff and cold.

The table was still overturned, the door still hanging open. There was no sound in the house. I boiled up the kettle and made myself a mug of tea. No one would be stirring in the Staithe yet. Soon I would switch on our flashing emergency light outside, our way of calling the mainland. Aunt Hetty would see it when she rose at six-thirty and would go to summon Bert.

I padded outside and looked about. The early mist had not yet dispersed. The low line of the mainland, with its woods and church towers, was obliterated. We might have been on an island out to sea. Nothing moved. I tried calling Tom, but there was no answer.

Somehow, I did not feel like venturing too far from the house, but I took a stout stick and walked towards The Feather. There I strolled with my feet in the wavelets, as common and lesser terns started up all round me. The tide was at its full. A boat was chugging up the channel.

The sound of that engine, the lines of the boat, and that figure in the blue jumper standing at the tiller, were all dearly familiar. It was Bert in his boat, amazingly, gratifyingly, early.

A moment later I saw he had a passenger. Not Dr Collins. Too early for her. It was Laura Ashworth.

I ran across to Cockle Bight, calling to them.

Soon Bert was helping her ashore. I caught his look of admiration as he gave her a hand. She was wearing the same clothes as last time I had seen her, a brown suede outfit. She gave me a big hug.

'What are you doing here?'

'I saw about the heart transplant on someone's television. I was in Spain, in the south. I got here as soon as I could.'

'Laura came up on the milk train from London,' said Bert admiringly.

'And got you out of bed, I see,' I said. But there were more important things to talk about. 'There's trouble, Bert. I know Tom's in fearful trouble.'

As quickly as I could, I told them both what had happened.

'I'll stay and help you find Tom,' Bert said. He tied up his boat and we headed back to the house.

'This new creature who's taken possession of Barry's body,' I said. 'It seems to think that all its life so far has been stolen from it. Now it wants to take over Tom's body as well. They are caught in some terrible battle I don't understand.'

'Another psychic battle! Poor Tom's been involved in a psychic battle all his life,' said Laura.

'It could be over today.' I told them about the hospital arrangements.

Laura had not slept all night. I made her some tea, and then we set out to search the Head. She and I set off together eastwards along the seaward side, Bert took the landward side.

We had the sun in our eyes. We said little to each other. Every now and again, we called Tom. I pictured him struggling with that new nameless thing, the evil face close against his, his feeling of absolute desperation. I longed to be with him. I longed for Laura to be with him.

After about two hours, we heard a distant shout. We

answered it. We stood where we were. Bert appeared over a distant dune, waving once. Immediately, I knew something was wrong. Laura and I looked into each other's faces and set off in Bert's direction.

His face was grim. As we came together, he took my hands without looking at Laura.

'Tom's over by the observation post, my love. Don't go.'

'I must go to him.'

'He's dead, love. Laura, you look after Robbie, will you? I'm going to get back to the boat fast as I can, and I'll come back with the police.'

He gave me a kiss and was off across the uneven ground at a jogtrot.

'I got to go to Tom,' I said.

She came with me.

The joined bodies lay on the landward side of the observation post. A bank of cobbles was piled against one side of the wooden hut and they lay together on the cobbles. All the way, I had been unable to believe Tom could be dead. Directly I saw him, I knew. The two joined bodies were huddled in positions the living never use.

Laura gave a cry and took a step ahead of me. She too stopped. You could go no nearer.

On the brow of the other head was a black and bloody contusion, where Tom had struck it with a stone. Tom's head was almost locked with Barry's.

His right hand still clutched a big scallop shell. After knocking the other out, he had performed an operation of his own. The other's naked chest had been cut to pieces by the scallop. Beside the frightful wound lay Barry's artificial heart. Tom had ripped it out of place after laying the chest open.

He must have died almost as soon as the other. The load on his heart would have been great. Now his frenzy was past. The lines of his face were relaxed. From his twisted position, one eye looked up into the morning sky.

Laura squatted down in front of him and began to weep.

These painful events have now receded into the past. How vividly I recall crouching by that mutilated double body, my knees painful on the cobbles, crying, and hearing the flies buzz.

Finally, Laura and I gathered ourselves up and went back along the strand. I summoned father. Later, Bert returned with a police officer. Bert took me and Laura away from the Head. The bodies followed later in another boat.

I never knowingly failed my two brothers. Perhaps I failed the other. Perhaps I could have helped him too.

Although I sometimes dream of him, those dreams have now shed their terror. His lost life – what did he think, experience . . . ? Was his a dream or a life? I don't know what to make of it, any more than I know what to make of anyone's life, come to that.

The days are full enough, now that I have children of my own. They too are making their journey through the forests of life. Sometimes when they are in bed, Bert and I play the old Bang-Bang LPs to ourselves. Then I look out of the window and across the waters, to where father still lives out his solitary life on L'Estrange Head. Everything vanishes in time, like the music when the record stops playing.

R.S.

Appendix

Big Lover

Go to my lover and say
   That Earth is nothing but a star,
It's just the merest light-point
   To even its nearest neighbours.

Serenade her with the facts
   Concerning life on Earth,
Its startling brevity of tenure
   Give her cosmology and music

To show her she is my lens
   Through which I view the universe,
My eye, my sun/My big lover
   My galactic one.

Love is a Forest

The animal and the sublime
   Make you so versatile,
You keep three lovers happy
   Yet torture them meanwhile.

In this world I'm love's tourist
   And take a package tour of solitude
Our love is a forest.

Oh you are all things to me
   Victim and vampire,
You keep three lovers happy
   A phoenix of their fire.

In this world I'm love's tourist
   Another head is dreaming of your beauty
Our love is a forest.

Your loveliness is legend,
   A statue I would carve,
You keep three lovers happy
   And satisfied to starve.

In this world I'm love's tourist
   Our love is a forest.

Bacterial Action

Although the world fills up with men
   Their numbers do not match
The numbers of the swarming swarms
   Of creatures living in our skin.
They have their nations and domains,
   Pleasant jungles, deserts, streams.
They live, beget, and leave no trace
   For eye to see or mind to judge.
They've no Byzantium or Rome,
   Yet they were there, in smock and gown;
Proud Caesar was their planet too,
   In time their old prolific line
Will speed commensally with us
   And all unknowing win the stars –
Yes, ultimately win the stars
         Unknowing

We – who had survived the journey
 To the forty-seventh millennium
Where dark starlight grows on bushes
And eyes house laughing kookaburra birds –
We sat drinking *xwaszha* in a café
With boys and beauties whose grandfathers
Were in their cots when we set out.
It was triumph
It was triumph
My happiness took me to loving hearts and couches
Yet we who had survived the journey
Knew that all the while our memory
Stayed with those elegant grey seas
Curling over what was Europe.

Just for a Moment

Just for a moment think about spun glass spinning
    Moving in a low December's sun,
Shining above rough dark secret meadows
    Lying where the leaf-choked marshes run.

Just for a moment think about a perfect colour
    Fading on the margins of the sea,
Lapping against a pallid shingle pathway
    Leading to a castle tall and free.

Just for a moment think about pure silence
    Shining above a distant mountain peak,
Looking towards the radiant eye of moonlight
    Falling upon the contours of your cheek.

Just for a moment visualize time absolute
   Dwelling through a planet's unlived years,
Passing over far untravelled tundras
   Turning where the long-haired comet steers.

Or just for a moment think about a moment
   Let movement colour silence time all flow,
About your lovely waiting head unknowing –
   And then you'll know my love's bounds,
           Then you'll know.

I Was Never Deaf or Blind to Her Music

No, I was never deaf or blind to your music, Laura

I breathed more oxygen in her company,
   Reached higher speeds and a wider sort of skies
And dredged for her secret salts and alkalis.

   It was just that the days closed in,
A new motorway went up between her place and mine.
We couldn't agree on the merits of Stockhausen
There were quarrels about my drinking habits
We stopped going to gigs together
And then there was that trouble with her employer
         Never properly explained
I started breeding wire-haired terriers
She said she lost her respect for me when
         I couldn't give up smoking.
But no, I was never impervious to her vistas
Plunging into the lake of what she was
She stormed me every day like valiant deeds
And my head was as full of her as poppy seeds.

It was just that the weather changed,
My job took me up Sheffield every week.
I felt a compulsion to join the scientologists
She got mad on Dresden china pieces
We became hooked on television
She suddenly wanted to see the Sierra Nevadas
            And dance the true Flamenco
With a bearded Dutchman studying zoology
When I think of her driving round Granada
            I long for our time again.

No, I was never deaf or blind to her music,
Time was, her alchemy was all upon me.
She packed every moment like a picnic box
She was air and sea to my hills and rocks.

I was never deaf or blind to your music, Laura.

WHERE THE LINES CONVERGE

Anna Macguire drove to see her father whenever she could. The opportunities grew fewer and fewer, although she knew he needed help. She said to herself, 'I go as often as I can because I love him as much as I am capable of doing, given the limitations of my nature. Since those limitations were to large extent fixed by the dreadful way he and my mother brought me up, then he has only himself to blame if I do not turn up as often as he would like.'

She had another excuse ready to explain why she went to Crackmore less often than formerly. Since the new airport had been built, Crackmore had become extremely difficult to reach. The old main road, the A394, had been severed. It ended at Ashmansford now, and a lengthy detour was needed, meandering through all the lesser roads skirting the west side of the airport. True, a new spur had been added between Packton and Bucklers Wick, but that was only useful for traffic approaching from the west. Then again, the fast new airport road ran really in the wrong direction. Anna had used it once, driving right into the airport and out again at the north side; but she had lost her direction and was forced to make a detour through Plough and North Baldick.

She had said to her boyfriend, as she called him, in one of her small flat jokes, 'It's all sort of symbolic of the way old people are cut off. Every time you improve a means of transport – i.e. build a new airport – you lose a generation. I'm sure Pop sees it that way.'

She actually said 'i.e.', as Trevor reported to his buddies in the office the next day. That was a Friday. By then, Anna, having scrounged a day off from the lab, was turning off just north of Ashmansworth, watching anxiously for the sign to Watermere.

Felix Macguire was due to retire from King Aviation Systems when the plan for the new airport was passed officially. Judy had been alive then.

'We'll be able to flog this property for twice what it's worth,' he said. 'How'd you like to go and live in the Algarve, my love?'

'I'm getting too old for change,' she said.

'We could swim nine months of the year.'

'I'm too old to get into a swimsuit,' she said.

He smiled at her then, as part of the plan he had carried out tenaciously for over thirty years to keep her as happy as possible, for his own sake, and said gallantly, 'I'd rather see you swimming in the nude.'

Eventually, the representative of a firm of land-developers came and made an offer for Macguire's house and gardens. The offer was disappointingly small.

Felix and Judy hung on for a bigger offer. 'We'll force them to improve their bid,' he said. 'We can wait as well as they can.'

They waited. They were only on the margins of the new development. A new offer never came. Felix wrote and accepted the old offer. The firm wrote back five weeks later (addressing the letter to P. McGuine) to say there was no longer any necessity to purchase the property referred to. Judy died before the first runway was completed.

The barriers of the airport came swinging along, mile after mile of green-plastic-clad chain-link unrolling, munched off the road that passed Macguire's drive, and strode over the ditch that drained his pathetic little piece of orchard. There was one house still occupied next to Macguire's, owned by a pleasant retired art-auctioneer called Standish who kept three Airedales. He had misplayed his hand much as

Felix had, and was stuck with deteriorating property. On the evening of the day that the fence went by his land, secured by an enormous roaring machine that spat ten-foot concrete fence posts into the ground at five metre intervals, Standish shot his dogs, poured petrol all over the ground floor of his house, lit it, ran upstairs to his bedroom, sat himself down at a desk before a faded portrait of himself as a little boy, and blew his brains out. Felix heard the shots, even above the roar of an SST coming in.

From then on, he let weeds grow in his garden and the beeches became shaggier in the drive. He stayed indoors, concentrating on developing an advanced system of vision screens he called the Omniviewer, and thinking about the growing inhumanity of man.

'Oh, piss!' said Anna. She steered the Triumph into the side of the road and pulled the map over to her. She had gone wrong somewhere. She didn't recognize this stretch of road at all. She should have been through Wainsley by now. The map remained inscrutable.

She climbed out and stood in the road. There was no traffic. Anonymous countryside all round. Being a townswoman, she could not tell whether or not the fields were properly tended. The only landmark was an old railway station down a lane, its ruined roof showing across the nearest field. No rails served this monument to an obsolete transport system. Huge elms choked by ivy stood everywhere; she watched a transport plane appear to blunder between them like a huge moth.

A man stood in front of her. He might have materialized out of the ground. She thought immediately, 'It's true, I wouldn't mind being raped, if we could go somewhere comfortable, but he might have all sorts of horrible diseases. And he might strangle me when he'd finished.'

But the man simply said, 'You aren't going to Casterham, are you?'

'No, I don't think so. I want to get to Crackmore. Do you know if I'm going the right way?'

He'd never heard of Crackmore. But he set her right for Wainsley, and she drove on again. At the last moment, she offered him a lift, but he refused; he wasn't going to be led on.

'I'm so isolated,' she said aloud, 'so isolated,' as she drove.

But she had to admit to herself that it was a half-hearted protest; after all, she could always have *asked* the man if she wanted it that badly. People did, these days.

The self-focusing cameras were his especial contribution. Light-and-motion-sensitive cells ensured that lenses focused on him whenever he entered a room. Working slowly, spending a generous part of every day out in the workshop-laboratory next to the disused garage, Felix built himself a spy system, which would record any movements within the house.

When he had a few thoughts to express, Felix uttered them aloud and the house swallowed them as a whale swallows plankton – and would regurgitate them later on request.

'The Omniviewer is designed purely for self-observation; it is introspective. All other spy systems have been extrovert, designed to watch other people. Their purposes have generally been malign. The parallel with the human senses is striking. Human beings are generally motivated throughout life to watch others and not themselves, right from the early days in which they begin to learn by imitation and example . . . I must remind the grocer when he calls that that last lot of tinned meat gave me diarrhoea.'

Leaving the workshop, he went through the garage into the hall, which he crossed, and entered the living-room. This he had bisected with partitioning some while ago, when he had been feeling his way towards a correct method of procedure for his experiments. It was in the far corner of the living-room, the south-pointing corner of the house, that he had built his main control console. The workshop contained an auxiliary console.

From the main console, he could direct the movements of the nine cameras situated about the house, mainly on the ground floor. On monitor screens before him, he could keep zealous eye on most corners of the house – and above all on himself. Several times, he had detected movements that roused – indeed, confirmed – his suspicions, and of these he kept careful note, recording place, time, and appearance and gesture of the alien pseudo-appearance. 'Alien pseudo-appearance' was his first, half joking, label for his early discoveries.

As usual, when he began work in the morning, he ran through a thorough check of all electronic equipment and sightings. That took him till noon. It was more than a check. It was a metaphysical exploration. It was a confirmation both of the existence of his world and of its threatened disintegration.

He switched the cameras on in turn, according to the numbered sequence he had given them, beginning with Number One. In this way, organization was held at maximum. Not until much later in the morning would he get round to testing Camera Nine, perched outside on the chimney-stack of the house – none of the other cameras, except Five and Three, were situated for looking beyond the confining walls; that was not their province.

As Camera One briefly warmed, a scatter of geometrical patterns flashed like blueprints across the small monitor, grew, grew, burst, and were instantly gone. An unwavering picture snapped into being on the tiny screen.

This camera was located on its pivot in the wall behind Felix and some two feet above his head. As it was at present directed, beamed downwards and ahead (he carefully read off its three-dimensional positioning on a calibrated control globe), it showed the control console itself,

113

with its switches and monitors, and Felix's right hand resting on the desk; the back of Felix's head was visible in one corner; so was the lower half of the partition, on which a giant viewing-screen had been erected. Also visible were the edge of the carpet, part of the wall, and a section of the window sill. The pattern on the monitor was a restful one of converging angles, relieved by the greater complexity covering about a third of the screen of the console.

Felix scrutinized the view in a leisurely and expert manner. In many ways, One always provided the most absorbing view, if not the most interesting perspectives.

After a thorough scrutiny, he switched on the large viewing-screen. Before viewing it direct, he watched it light in the monitor-screen, via One.

The scatter of particles cleared and the tiny screen showed him the lower strip of the large screen, on which part of the console with the monitors was visible. On Number One of these tiny monitors, he could see the image of the lower strip of the large screen, with its line-up of monitors on the console. On the first of those monitors was a blur of light which the definition, however good, would not resolve into a clear image. Better lenses were probably the answer there, and he was working on that.

Satisfied at last with optical details, he set the camera controls to Slow Scan.

Camera One had a scan of two hundred and ten degrees laterally and little less in the vertical axis. Among the many pleasures of its field of vision – to be taken in due turn – was the view at 101·40 N, 72·50 W, which gave the corner of the room, where the south-east and south-west walls of the house met at the ceiling, as well as an oblique glimpse of the right-hand of the two windows in the front (south-east) wall. The merging and diverging lines were particularly significant, and there was the added pleasure of the paradox that although almost all the windows could be seen, the view was so oblique that little could be observed beyond the window, except an insignificant stretch of weedy gravel; this seemed to reduce the window to a properly auxiliary status.

Also desirable, and considerably more complex, was the view at 10·00 N, 47·56 E. It gave one insignificant corner of the console, looking over it towards one of the two doors in the L-shaped room which led into the hall passage. Through this door, the camera took in a dark section of the passage, the doorway of the dining-room beyond, and a segment of the dining-room including a bit of the table with a chair pushed in to it (the dining-room was never used), the carpet, a shadowy piece of ceiling, something of one of the two windows, and Camera Six, which stood on a bracket set in the wall at a height slightly less than that of One. 10·00 N, 47·50 E became even more engrossing when Six was functioning, since it then showed One in action; and, when One was in motion, its slight and delicate action was the only observable movement.

There were automatic as well as manual controls for each camera, so that 'favourite' or 'dangerous' or 'tranquil' views could be flicked over to at a moment's notice. There were also programmed automatics, by means of which the eight indoor cameras ran through a whole interrelated series of sightings of high complexity and enfiladed the entire volume of the house – for Felix had his moments of panic, when the idea that he had caught an unsuspecting movement, a figure all too like his own, would send his adrenalin count rocketing and his heart pounding, and he would snap into a survey of the whole territory. His recording system allowed him to play back and study any particular view at leisure.

Frequently, he saw shots which filled him with grave doubt, as he played them back and allowed his heart-rate to ease. Although no figures were revealed – his opponents were very clever – their presence was often implied by shadows, dark smudges, mingled fans of light and shade on carpet. They were there, right enough, meddling deliberate-

115

ly; and although no doubt some of the discrepancies in the visual record could be ascribed to aircraft passing low overhead, they were unwise to think he would always use that excuse as a pretext for believing in their non-existence.

When he had thoroughly tested out Camera One through its entire sphere of scan, Felix left it running – and it would run now until he closed down after midnight – and switched on Camera Two.

Camera Number Two was on the far wall of the workshop. It had been the first of the series of cameras to be installed. It overlooked the length of the narrow workshop, including the screens of the auxiliary console, and the door at the far end, which always stood open (not only for security reasons but because the coaxial cable running to the rest of the house prevented its closure) to give a view into the garage, piled high with its old grocer's cartons and crates of video tape.

Although none of the cameras offered a very colourful scene, Two gave the greyest one. As, under Felix's control, it commenced its slow scan, it had nothing bright to show, although, rolling towards the roof like an upturning eye, it picked up a patch of blue sky through the reinforced glass skylight.

When it lit obliquely on the three blown-up photographs on the inner wall, Felix slowed the motor until the view was almost steady and stared with satisfaction at the images of the photographs thrown on the big screen before him. There he saw three gigantic sea-going creatures, each remarkably similar to the next in its functional streamlined form. Something of his original thrill of horror and discovery came back to him as he looked.

He said aloud: 'My evolutionary discovery is greater than Charles Darwin's, or his grandfather's . . . greater and far more world shaking. Darwin revealed only part of the truth, and that revelation has ever since concealed a far greater and more awesome truth. Do you hear me out there?

I have the patience and courage of Charles Darwin . . . I too will wait for years if necessary, until I have incontrovertible proof of my theories.'

Still staring at the images of the photographs, he switched to playback. He sat listening to his own voice, filtering softly through the house.

'—man beings are generally motivated throughout life to watch others and not themselves, right from the early days in which they begin to learn by imitation and example . . . I must remind the grocer when he calls that that last lot of tinned meat gave me diarrhoea . . . My evolutionary discovery is greater than Charles Darwin's . . .'

He heard himself out and then added, 'The proof is mounting slowly.'

He smiled at the pictures. They were more than a statement of faith; they were a defiance of the enemy. In truth, he inwardly cared little for his own bombast broadcast through the silent and possibly unoccupied rooms; yet it gave him a certain courage – and courage was needed at all times by all who moved towards the unknown – and of course it had a propaganda value. So he sat quietly, breathing regularly under his tattered sweater, as he watched the viewpoint of Two crawl lethargically past the marine shapes and up the formless areas of wall.

When Anna reached what was left of Crackmore, the morning was well advanced. She stopped the car at the filling station and got petrol. She had a headache and a sniffy nose. The pollen count was high, the midsummer heat close about her temples.

'Oh God, don't say I'm going to get one of my streaming colds! What a bore!'

With a feeling of oppression, she saw as she left the untidy station that the village had entered a phase of new and ugly growth. A big filling station was under construction not a hundred metres away from the one at which she had

117

stopped. Next to it, a poky estate of semi-detacheds was going up. A new road to the connecting road to the airport was being built, cutting through what was left of the old village. Although, admittedly, the old village was nothing to get excited about, at least it had preserved a sense of proportion, had been agreeably modest in scale. Now a gaunt supermarket was rising behind the old square, dwarfing the church. Everywhere was cluttered and uncomfortable. She was amazed – as so often before – at how many people showed a preference for an inhuman environment. As she drove by the road-making machines, a jet roared overhead, reminding her of her headache.

'Piss off!' she told it.

It was so senseless. There could now be nobody remaining in Crackmore who desired to live there. Most of them would be attached to the ground staff of the airport or something similar, and lived where they did purely for financial interest. Anyone with any spark of humanity in them had fled from the area long ago.

She turned off by the old war memorial ('Faithful Unto Death' 1914–18, 1939–45) and headed towards her father's house. The road shimmered in its own heat, creating imaginary pools and quagmires into which she drove.

Round the last corner, she passed the burnt-out shell of the Standish mansion. Burdock grew along its drive, rusty with July, and eager green things had sprung up round what was left of the structure. Sweet rocket flowered haphazardly. The shade under the high beeches behind was as dark as night. Ahead, lopping off the road, the airport fence. The fence put a terminator on everything – beyond was only the anticyclonic weather, breaking into slaty cumulus, which began to pile up the sky like out-of-hand elms, growing above low cloud and threatening a chance of thunder before the afternoon died.

The drive gates stood open. As the Triumph turned in, Anna saw that the drab green fence was closer to her father's

118

house than she recalled. It was too long since she last visited Felix; her neglect of him was part of a greater neglect, of the wastage of everything.

On the other side of the fence, the road had been eradicated; machines had wiped it out of existence; on this side of the fence, nature was at work doing the same thing, throwing out an advance guard of wild grasses and buttercup, following up with nettles, dock, thistles, and brambles. Soon they would come sprawling their way along the road. It needed only a year or two, and they would be at the house.

Anna drew up before the front door, noting how the trees about the drive, beech and copper beech, had grown more ragged and encroached more since she was last here. She blew her nose before climbing out, not wishing her father to suspect she might have a cold developing.

The house had been solidly built just after the turn of the century, with grey slate roof and red brick, and a curious predilection for stone round the windows. It had never been fashionable or imposing, though perhaps aiming at both; nevertheless, even in its old neglected age, it manifested something of the rather flashy solidity of the epoch in which it had been designed and constructed.

Before entering, Anna let a certain dread provoke her into stepping across the weedy gravel to peer through the living-room windows. Through the second window, she saw her father crouched in his swivel chair, looking fixedly at something beyond the range of her vision. She stared at him as at a stranger. Felix Macguire was still a powerful man, the lines of his face were still commanding, while the recessing of his gums lent more emphasis than at any other stage in his life to a determined line of chin and jaw. His white hair, hanging forward over his brow, still contained something of the boisterousness she recalled in her childhood. All in all, he, like the house, had weathered well, retaining the same flashy solidity of the Edwardian Age.

Feeling guilty for spying on him, she turned away, thinking in a depressed way that her father seemed scarcely changed in appearance from when she could first remember him in childhood; yet she herself no longer had youthful expectations of life, and was moving towards middle age. With her habitual quick shift of thought, she ironically pronounced herself resigned to her own listless company.

She tried the handle of the front door. It opened. Hinges squeaked as she entered the hall.

Despite the heat outside, the feeling in the house was one of cold and damp; a comfortlessness less physical than an attribute of the phantoms haunting it. But the lengths of coaxial cable running boldly over the carpet or snaking up the stairs, the doors – to garage, lavatory, coat cupboard, and living-room – wedged open, all contributed to the discomfort – not to mention the slow stare of Camera Four, situated knee-high on its bracket on the corner of the coat cupboard, where it could survey front door, hall, passage, and stairs.

'Are you there, Father? It's me, Anna.'

She went down the passage and through the second door of the living-room. He had risen from the console and stood awaiting her. She went over to him and kissed him.

'How are you? You're looking well! Why didn't you write or send me a few words on a tape! I've been worried. I'm sorry it's been so long since my last visit, but we've been terribly busy at the labs – trade's bad, and that always seems to mean more work, for me at least. I had to go up to Newcastle with one of the partners last weekend or I would have come over then. Did you get my card, by the way? I'm sure I've sent you that view of the Civic Hall before, but it seemed to be the only view they had at the tobacconist's . . .'

She paused and her father said, 'It's good of you to bother to come at all, Anna. I'll get you a cup of coffee, or something, shall I?'

'No, no, I'll get it. That's what I'm here for, isn't it?

120

And may I open a window or two? It's terribly stuffy in here – it is July, you know, and you need some warm air circulating. And why don't you keep the front door locked when you are alone in the house? Suppose someone broke in?'

'If the front door is unlocked, I can get out quicker if I need to, can't I?'

They stared at each other. Anna dropped her gaze first.

'You aren't exactly welcoming, are you, Father?'

'I said it was good of you to come. I'm pleased to see you. But it's no good complaining about the way I live directly you get in the house.'

'I'm sorry, Father, really. I didn't mean to nag, of course. Just a motherly instinct – you know what women are!' She put on a smile and moved to embrace him, then clumsily cut off the gesture. 'Father, you're alone far too much. I know what you think about me, but you don't make it easy – you've never made it easy. Even when I was a little girl and I used to run to you—'

'You are grown up now, Anna!'

'Oh God, don't rub it in! You took care of that! What does being grown up mean but being even more isolated than as a child? What made you so inhuman, Father? You never really loved me, did you? Why do you still expect me to come all this way up here to visit you, and it's terribly difficult to get here, just to make fun of me?'

'I don't expect you to visit me, Anna. You have to come now and then just to reproach me. You know very well that what you say hurts. You have in some way failed to achieve a mature personality and so you blame me for that. Perhaps I am to blame. But what use is blame? Was it worth coming this far just to deliver it?'

'Nothing's of any use to you, is it?' she said sulkily. 'I'll go and make coffee, if there's any in the house.'

Her father went back to sit down before his monitor screens. He switched Camera Eight on to the big screen and sat looking at an image of the inner wall of the second bedroom which included part of a wardrobe and, hanging from the picture rail, an engraving of Sir Edward Poynter's 'Faithful Unto Death', which had belonged to his mother.

In a minute, Anna poked her head round the door.

'Coffee's ready! Come and have it in the kitchen – it's a bit fresher in here.'

He went through and took the cup she offered him. Anna had opened the door to the side drive. Sunlight lay there in patches between trees.

'I'm pleased to see you have plenty of provisions in the house. At least you keep yourself fed properly. Prices of everything keep going up and up. I don't know where it will all end.'

'I live very comfortably, Anna. I nourish myself, I exercise myself. I am entirely dedicated to my research and mean to keep myself as healthy as possible in order to pursue it. Did you manage to get the volume on convergence by Krost?'

'No, not yet. Foyle's had to order specially, and still it hasn't come through. Sorry. Everything takes so long. How's the research going?'

'Steadily.'

'I know you aren't very keen to tell me about it, but you know I'm interested. Perhaps I could be of more help to you if you would tell me a bit more.'

'My dear, I appreciate your interest, but I've told you before – the work has to be secret. I don't want it blabbed about and, in the sphere in which I'm working, you could not possibly be of any help.'

'Ignoring the insulting suggestion that I should blab your secrets everywhere, couldn't I approach someone—'

'You know what I mean, you might tell one of your boy friends casually—' He paused, knowing he had said the wrong thing, blinked, and said hastily, 'You shall have, perhaps, a small demonstration of what I'm doing. But I

122

must keep it all secret. I'm on the brink of something extra-ordinary, that I know ... one of those discoveries – revelations – that can completely overturn the thinking of all men, as Galileo did when he turned his telescope to the sky. There were telescopes, there was sky. But *he* was the man who had the original thought, *he* was the man who looked in a new direction. I am doing that. To you – though you may be my daughter – I'm just an old eccentric, spending his days staring at television screens. Aren't I, admit it?! Well, that's much what they thought of Galileo ... The name of Felix Macguire, my child ... a few more years ... I can't tell you ...'

'Don't let your coffee get cold, Father.'

He turned his back to her and stared out of the door at the unkempt bushes.

'I understand, Father. I mean, I understand your aspirations. Everyone has them. I know I have.'

Her pathetic words, intended to contain a charge of reassurance through shared experience, died on her lips. In a more practical voice, she said, 'All the same, it's not good for you to live here alone like this. I don't like it. It's a responsibility for me. I want you to come and live near me in Highgate where I can keep an eye on you ... Or, if you won't do that, then I want a medical friend of mine to be allowed up here to see you. Robert Stokes-Wallis. He's a follower of Laing's. Perhaps you know his name.'

She sniffed and blew her nose. Felix turned and watched her performance.

'I warn you, Anna, I want no interference with my routine. Tell your man to stay away. You think I'm cranky. Maybe I am. It's a cranky world. Whether I'm mad or not is really a question of no importance beside the magnitude of the questions I am confronting. Now, let's say no more on that subject.'

'Drink your coffee,' she said pettishly. 'And what's this demonstration you want to give me?'

Felix picked up the mug and sipped. 'Are you, in fact, particularly interested?'

Making an effort, she laid a hand on the arm of his sweater. 'I'm sure that you understand that I really am interested, Father, and always have been, when allowed to be. I am really quite an intelligent and loving creature to my friends. So of course, I am keen to see your demonstration.'

'Good, good. You need only say yes – speeches aren't necessary. Now, I don't want you to be disappointed by the demonstration, because there is a danger it may seem very flat to you, you understand? Let me explain something about it first.'

He pulled a book off the top of the refrigerator.

'Milton's poems. "Paradise Lost". I read it sometimes when I'm not working. A marvellous poem, although it contains a view of reality as a theological drama to which we no longer subscribe. When Milton was in Italy, he visited Galileo Galilei, and something of the astronomer's involvement with the heavens has got into the poem. Galileo is the greater man, because the scientist must take precedent over the poet; but either must have a measure of the other for real greatness.'

'Father, you forget that you read me most of Book IV of "Paradise Lost" last time I came up here. It is not my favourite poem.'

' "What seest thou else in the dark backward and abysm of time?" Let me come to the point, which is not exactly Milton. We are talking about views of reality to which we no longer subscribe. The geocentric view of the universe prevailed for over a thousand years – needlessly, since a heliocentric view had been advanced before that. How can anything be correctly understood when such a great thing is misunderstood? It was not just a minor astronomical error – it was grounded in Man's erroneous view of his own importance in the universe.

'Nobody believes in the Ptolemaic geocentric view nowadays, and yet nevertheless thousands – millions of people have found a way of clinging to that ancient error by maintaining a belief in astrology: that the movements of remote suns can control a human destiny, or that, vice versa, human behaviour can provoke eclipses or similar signs of heavenly displeasure. Clear views of reality are at a premium. Indeed, I've come to believe something always distorts our vision. Bacon comes very close to the same conclusions in his "Novum Organum".

'Take mankind's idea of its own nature. In the west, the view prevailed until the nineteenth century that we were God's creatures, especially made to act in some obscure drama of His making. Your grandmother believed in the tale of Adam and Eve, and in every word of Genesis. She preferred that version of reality to Darwin's. Darwin showed that we were different from the animals only in degree and not in kind. But the opposite view had prevailed practically unchallenged for centuries, and men still prefer to behave as if they were apart from Nature. Not only is the truth hard to come by – it's often refused when available.'

'I see that but, surely, in this century we have had our noses rubbed in reality uncomfortably enough.'

'I don't think so, Anna. I believe we have escaped again. Look at the way in which the so-called side effects of technology are universally deplored. Everyone who pretends to any degree of civilization agrees to condemn nuclear warfare, the pollution of air, sea, and land, the sort of dreadful fate that has overtaken Crackmore, the hideous tide of automobiles which chokes our cities. Yet all these things are brought about by us. We have the power over technological and legislative processes to end all such abuses tomorrow if we wished. Instead, we continue to stock-pile nuclear weapons, we go on making thousands of automobiles per day, we continue to destroy every accessible environment. Why? Why? Because we wish it. Because we *like* it that way, because we crave disaster. That is the truth – that we think

125

we feel otherwise is yet another proof of how incapable mankind is of coping with reality.'

'Oh, but to argue like that – that's silly, Father! After all, growing numbers of people—'

'I know what you are going to say—'

'Oh, no, you don't—'

'I know what you are going to say. You are going to say that there are increasing numbers of people who are showing by action that they hate what technology is doing to us. Perhaps. I do not suggest all men feel the same. Indeed, part of my thesis is that man is divided. But by and large there is a mass wish for catastrophe, hidden under mass delusion. So a considerable amount of my time here is devoted to bringing reality under better control.'

She shook her head. 'Father, honestly, you just can't—'

He shut the door to the drive. 'We must bring reality under control. The technology we turn against ourselves can be turned to fortify that weak link in our brains which always seeks to deceive us about our own natures! I'll show you how. You've had the lecture – now the demonstration. Go and sit in the other room at my chair and watch Number Five monitor screen.'

Putting his hands on her shoulders, he guided her from the kitchen. He noticed how stiff and lifeless her body felt, and hurriedly removed his hands. In time to catch the expression on his face, Anna turned and said, 'Father, I do want to be of help to you – desperately! It's awful how people in families get all tangled up with their relationships, but I do want to be more of a dau—'

'Demonstration first!' he said, briskly, pushing her forward. 'Get in there and sit patiently watching Monitor Five. That's all you have to do.'

Sighing, she went through into the living-room. Most of its original furniture had been pushed back into one corner.

An old sofa covered the unused fireplace. There were cushions, occasional tables, a magazine rack, and an old box piled on top of the sofa. The room had been further reduced in meaning by the partition across it, with the television screen burning on it. Past the side of the partition, she could see through the other door of the room and out through the discomfort of the hall, the eye perforce following the intertwined snakes of black cable, into the garage, with its empty crates and wall of breeze blocks.

She sat at the console, took a tissue out of her handbag, and blew her nose. The headache was there in full force, despite two aspirins she had swallowed with her coffee. The atmosphere was leaden.

On the large screen burned an image which she recognized as one of the bedrooms, although it was years since she had been upstairs. Despite herself, she was interested and, as she scrutinized the picture, tried to reason why she should be. She could see through an open door to a landing across which light and ill-defined shadows of banisters lay, to a corner of wall; the continuation of landing had to be deduced from the chiaroscuro eclipsed by the bedroom doorpost. From this glimpse, Anna deduced she was seeing a view from the spare bedroom at the top of the stairs.

Inside the room, she could see the foot of a bed, part of a wardrobe, and a picture hanging against a patterned wallpaper. She leaned forward instinctively, interested to see if the bed were made up. It appeared not to be. She also stared at the picture on the wall. A man, perhaps a soldier, was holding a pike or a spear and gazing fearfully upwards at the entrance to a forbidding alley; behind him, something awful was going on; but she could make little of it.

All, on the surface, was dull and without any power to enchant; yet she felt herself enchanted.

The colours were of high quality, conveying an impression

127

that they were true to reality but perhaps enhanced it slightly. For instance, the landing carpet: mauve: but did it actually present those tender lavender contrasts between shadowed and unshadowed strips? Or was it that the colours on the screen were true and one merely paid them a more attentive respect because they were images of the real thing? Was there an art about the reproduction that the reality lacked?

She noted belatedly that the sound was on, so that she was actually listening to this silent vista as well as watching it. And she noted something else: that the viewpoint was low, as if the camera was fixed just above the skirting. So one was forced into the viewpoint more of a child than an adult. That might explain why the shadows radiating from the wardrobe seemed both somewhat emphatic and somewhat menacing, as well as accounting for some of the fascination of the picture as a whole.

But was it a live picture or a still? Anna was convinced it was no still. Some quality about it suggested a second-by-second congruence with her own life. Yet how to be sure? Of course, a long enough vigil would reveal movement in the shadows, or a diminution in light towards evening; but she found herself looking for a spider crossing her field of vision, perhaps a fly trapped in the room, circling vaguely under an overhead lampshade. Nothing moved.

With an involuntary shiver, she thought, 'That room's as lifeless as the top of Everest! It's not a real room any more – it's just a fossil!' Her attraction changed to revulsion and she looked down at the row of monitor screens to obey her father's directions.

Eight of the nine small screens were lit. All showed static views of rooms and, in the eighth, she saw duplicated – in miniature and in black-and-white – the view projected on the big screen. Its smallness gave it an even more hypnotic quality. It frightened her. As she averted her eyes, she caught sight of her father in the fifth screen, moving purposefully across it. Almost as soon as he was lost to sight on that screen, he was caught advancing in Number One screen, coming from a shadowy passage, and then he materialized in the room in person.

'Did you watch closely? What did you make of the demonstration?' he asked.

She stood up, vexed with herself.

'I was so fascinated with the view on the big screen . . . I was only just about to watch Number Five monitor.'

Felix frowned and shook his head. 'Such a simple thing I asked you to do—'

'Do the demonstration again, Father. I will watch this time, honestly! I'm sorry!'

'No, no, it was just a small thing, as I warned you. To do it after this fuss would make it meaningless.'

'Oh, no, that can't be so, surely. I wasn't making a fuss. I won't find it meaningless. You didn't give me enough time. You didn't give me a proper chance—' To her own dismay she began to cry. Angrily she turned her back on him, fumbling in her bag for a tissue.

'Always these overheated personal nonsenses!' Felix shouted. 'Isn't it enough that you should have been stupid without compounding it by bursting into tears? Dry your eyes, woman! – You're as bad as your mother!'

At that, she cried the louder.

When she turned round at length, he had left the room.

She stood there in a melancholy containment, with the unwinking monitors by her right hand. Should she leave, despite her headache, so much worse after the fit of weeping? Did he expect her to leave? And how much did his expectations influence whether she would actually leave or not?

In any case, it was past lunch time. She could either rustle up something from the kitchen, where she had found a surprisingly well-maintained range of food, or she could go down to the pub in Crackmore. She had meant to take him along to the pub, but his insufferable behaviour put a different aspect on things.

She glanced at the screens to see if she could catch sight of him. The view on Number Seven monitor was moving slowly; she looked and realized that the movement of the camera was automatic. The screen showed another bedroom, evidently her father's from its state of occupation. There was a cupboard, one door half-open to reveal suits within, and an untidy pile of clothes on a chair. She supposed the laundry man still called every week. The bed was unmade. The viewpoint was moving beyond it in a slow arc, taking in blank wall, an angle between walls complex with diffused shadow, then a window – seen obliquely, but revealing the tops of unkempt trees in the drive by the front gate – then the wall between windows, then the next window, rolling gently into view . . . No father there.

He had built neat switchboards; she realized that everything could be controlled from here. If she could set all the cameras tracking, then presumably she would detect him in one of the rooms. Tentatively, she pressed one of the piano keys nearest to her.

His voice came out at her. '—st lot of tinned meat gave me diarrhoea . . . My evolutionary discovery is greater than Charles Darwin's or his grandfather's . . . greater and far more world shaking. Darwin revealed only part of the truth—'

She switched him off.

He was mad. No doubt of it. Madness suited him – there had always been a madness in the distance he had kept between himself and everyone else.

He was probably dangerous too. Men with monomania were generally violent when opposed. She'd better be careful. But she'd always been careful. And really – she told herself in the thick ticking room – she had hated him since childhood.

She saw him on Number Four screen. He must have

rushed outside to avoid her crying; now he was entering the house, turning to close the door – my God, was locking it! Locking it! What did he mean to do?

Anna ran out of the nearer living-room door and into the kitchen. Panic momentarily overcame her. She ran across the kitchen and pulled open the door. Surely he was intending to trap her, or else why lock the front door? He had said he never locked it – What was the ghastly phrase? – 'If I don't lock up, I can escape faster'? Nutty as a fruit cake!

She ran from the kitchen. The gravel outside had sprouted so many weeds, so much grass, that it hardly showed any more. She hurried through them, thinking she had better get to her car and clear off, or at least go and get a drink and then return, cautiously, and plead with him to let Stokes-Wallis examine him . . . As she turned the corner and came to the front of the house, her father emerged from the front door and – no, it was not a run – *hastened* to her car.

Anna stopped a few yards away.

'What are you playing at, Father?'

'Are you going already, Anna?'

She went a little nearer.

'You aren't trying to stop me leaving, are you?'

'You are leaving, then, are you?' His hair almost concealed his eyes.

She paused.

'It's best if I leave, Father. I don't understand your work, you refuse to explain it to me, and I interrupt it in any case. It's not just a question of that, either, is it? I mean, there's the question of temperament, too, isn't there? We've never got on. It was your business – the way I look at it – to get on with me if you could, since I was your daughter, your only child, but, no, you never fucking well cared, did you? I was just an intrusion between you and Mother. Okay, then I'll get out, and as far as I'm concerned you can sit and goggle at your empty screens till you fall dead. Now get out of my way!'

As she came forward, Felix stepped back from the car. He let his gaze drop so that his eyes were completely hidden by the overhanging lock of his hair. His arms hung by his side. In his stained grey trousers and his torn sweater, he looked helpless and negative.

Proud of her victory, Anna marched forward and grasped the door handle of the Triumph. As she pulled it open, he seized her fiercely from behind, locking his arms round her so that her elbows were pinned against her sides.

She yelled in fright. A passenger jet roared overhead, taking up and drowning the note of her cry while he spun her round and dragged her into the house.

Even in her fury and fear, she found time to curse herself for forgetting that mannerism of her father. How often as a child had she seen him doing as he did then, suddenly turning deceptively limp and passive before springing on her like an enemy! She should not have been deceived! – But of course memory so often worked to obliterate the miseries of reality!

Once he had got her into the hall, he pulled her towards the side door into the garage. Anna recovered her wits and kicked backwards at his legs. He was immensely strong! Together, they tripped over the cables in the entrance and half-fell down the concrete step into the garage. As she broke from his grip, he caught her again and momentarily they were face to face.

'You're the enemy!' he said. 'You're one of the non-humans!'

Above their heads were unpainted wood shelves, crude-ly fixed to the wall with brackets and loaded with boxes and spools of plastic covered wire. Pinning his daughter to the wall, Felix reached up and dragged down one of the spools. The action tumbled a couple of boxes, and nails cascaded over their heads. Tugging savagely at her, Felix com-menced to bind her round and round with wire, securing her ankles as well as her wrists.

He was just finishing when they heard a distant knocking. Felix straightened. He pushed his hair from his eyes.

'That'll be the grocer. Don't make a sound, Anna, or I'll be forced – well, you know what I'll be forced to do!' He gave her a hard straight look which included no recognition of her as a human being.

As soon as he had got into the hall and was making for the kitchen, from which the knocking came, Anna struggled upright and hobbled towards the door. It was impossible to climb up the step into the hall with her ankles bound; she fell up it. Before she was on her feet again, her father was coming back. He had a letter in his hand, and was smiling.

'A Glasgow postmark – this will be from Professor Nicholson! The grocer kindly brings my mail along from the post office. He's a good fellow. He recognized your car; I told him I was having the pleasure of a visit from you. Now, my dear, we are going to get you upstairs. If you help yourself a bit, it won't be so painful.'

'Father, what are you going to do with me? *Please* let me go! I'm not a little girl any more, to be punished when I disobey your orders.'

He laughed. 'No, you are far from being a little girl, Anna. Just how far, I intend to discover for myself.'

She stared at him in shock, as if for the first time the helplessness of her position was made real to her. He read her expression and laughed again, a lot less pleasantly.

'Oh, no, my dear, I didn't mean what you think – whatever fantasies you entertain in the depths of your mind!'

'You don't know what I'm thinking!'

'I don't want to know what you're thinking! What a miserable generation yours was, obsessed by sex, yet totally unable to come to terms with your own sexuality. Your mother and I had a far better time than you or any of your friends will ever have!'

By dint of pushing and lifting, he got her upstairs and trundled her past the bathroom into the bedroom whose door stood open opposite the head of the stairs. She found herself in a bedroom at the back of the house, recognizing it indifferently as the room she had seen on the viewing screen.

'Now!' he said, looking round frowning.

He loosed some of the wire from her ankles, led her over to the bed, and tied her legs to the bedpost, so that she was forced to sit there. Then he disappeared. She heard him going downstairs. A minute later, he was back, a tenon saw on one hand. He knelt by the door and started to saw low down on the leading edge. When he had got six inches in, he stood and kicked vigorously at the bottom of the door. The wood splintered and a piece sagged outward. He kicked at it until it was loose.

The door would now shut, despite the cables trailing over the floor. Looking meaningfully at her once, he went out, and she heard him turning the key in the lock. She was properly imprisoned.

Impotently listening, she heard him march downstairs. Silence, then the sound of the Triumph engine starting up. What a fool she was to have left the key in the ignition – by no means for the first time! But he could always have taken the key from her bag; she had left it in the kitchen.

She heard the car engine fade almost immediately; so he had driven it round the side of the house, parking it beyond the kitchen door, where it would not be noticed from the road.

The grocer might see it when he called again – but how long ahead would that be? Evidently no postman called – the grocer had agreed to deliver her father's post. Perhaps no other tradesmen came up this cul-de-sac; her father might well rely on the friendly grocer for all supplies. Of course, she had told Trevor and some of the fellows in the labs where she was going, but Trevor was not to be relied on, while the rest of them would not give her another thought until Monday, when she did not show up for work. She was on her own.

Well, that was nothing new. It was just that the situation was more extreme than usual.

Anna was already working to free her hands. It should be possible. She had already noticed that her father had left – carelessly or by design? – the saw on the floor by the door. It might come in useful.

The front door slammed.

Of course, he could watch her over the Omniviewer. She glared across the room at the dull lens of the camera, bracketed in the wall against the disused grate, a foot above floor level. She would just have to hope that he was unable to watch all the time.

Her feet were less tightly tied than her wrists and arms. After working away carefully, she managed to slip one of her brogues off, and then to wriggle her stockinged foot from the coils. The other one came out easily, and she could walk round the room.

Still pulling at her wrists, she ran over to the window and looked out.

Clouds had piled up in the sky. The afternoon was torpid. She was looking over what had once been a vegetable garden. Impenetrable weeds grew there. They stopped at the high wire fence, drab green and stretching away into the distance. Beyond the fence lay the airport, flat and featureless. She could see no building from this window, only a distant plane, deserted on a runway.

The view was blank and alien. It offered her no courage.

Hooking her wrists over the catch of the window, she pulled and wriggled to such effect that in a minute her hands were free. As she rubbed her hands together, she listened for his footstep on the stair.

Just how dangerous was he? She could not estimate.

That he was her father made it all more difficult to calculate, more bizarre. If he came up, would he not, this time – at last – put his arms around her and love and forgive her for all her shortcomings?

No, he bloody well wouldn't!

The door was locked, as expected.

Anna crossed to the single picture on the wall above the bed, a sepia reproduction mounted and set in a solid oak frame. As she pulled it down, she saw that it represented a Roman sentry in armour standing guard before a gateway leading into a luridly lit court in which people were dying and dead – flares of some kind were falling from the skies on to them. The picture was called 'Faithful Unto Death'. She swung it in front of the camera, propping it against a chair so that the view was obstructed. Then she opened the window and looked out.

Felix Macguire was standing among the weeds aiming a gun of some kind at her. A rifle, possibly. Aimed at her. Half-fainting, she sank back inside the room.

Leaning against the wall, she heard him shouting. She began listening to his words.

'I'd have fired if you'd tried to jump. I warn you, Anna! You may not fully understand the situation, but I do. The fact that you are my daughter makes no difference. You are not going to leave here, or not until I say you can. Professor Basil Nicholson is coming tomorrow, and I want him to look at you. Behave yourself and you'll come to no harm. If you don't behave yourself, I'll lock you in the landing cupboard without food. Forget you're my daughter – remember you're my captive. Now, then – shut that window. Do you hear, shut the window?!'

She summoned enough presence of mind to look out and say, though without all the spirit she hoped for, 'Try and realize what you are saying and doing, Father! You are now formally renouncing me as your daughter, which is what you have wished to do all your life. You are also threatening to shoot me!'

He said angrily, 'This is a French carbine, used against rioters. I'll fire if you don't get back. I mean every word.' A few drops of rain began to fall.

'I'm sure you do! I don't doubt that. I'm sure you do! I'm sure you'd love to fire. But you should recognize what it means. You have now crossed the dividing line between sanity and madness. You are also committing a criminal act!'

'Get your head inside and close—' His words were drowned by the roar of an airliner coming in to land, but his threatening gestures were enough for her. Anna pulled her head back and wearily shut the window. She laid down on the bed and tried to think what she should do. Her stomach rumbled like thunder.

It was a problem to understand how matters between them had deteriorated so rapidly. Was it just because she had forgotten to watch his demonstration on the monitor, or because of some other fault of which she was unaware? And what had the demonstration been? Something minor, despite its build-up, that was clear: perhaps merely watching her father in the kitchen over the closed-circuit. Instead, she had been hooked into watching an empty room – this room. 'Getting control of reality': that had been his phrase. Had he, her all-powerful and untouchable father, been rewarded for his years of isolation – whether unwished for or self-imposed – by some amazing insight into the physical conditions governing man? Had he really stumbled on an equivalent to Galileo's proof of the heliocentric system? It was not past the bounds of credibility – but nothing was past the bounds of credibility these days. And if he had so done, he would naturally be impatient (though *impatient* was scarcely the word) with any silly girl who failed to follow him closely when he attempted to explain.

She lay looking up at the ceiling. She could hear rain

outside, and another slight sound. The camera was still working.

Warmth and comfort overcame her. Perhaps the aspirins were taking effect; her headache had gone. She began to recall summer days in their old house, before she had grown up, when her mother was alive, and she had lain as she was now lying on her bed, idly reading a book; the window was open to the summer breezes, and she could hear her parents down in the garden, exchanging an odd sentence now and again. Her mother was gardening, her father working on a monograph on lacunae in the theory of evolution which never got published. Evolutionary theory was always his hobby – a complete contrast from the pushing world of electronics into which his job took him. She had put her book down and gone over – yes, she had been barefoot – gone over to the window and looked out. He had waved to her and called something . . .

'Can you hear me, Father? I didn't mean to miss your demonstration, whatever it was, if that is why you're punishing me. If possible, I'd like to understand and help. It could be that when watching the big screen I had a useful insight into what you meant about reality. A view over the screen is different in some undefined way to a view direct, isn't it?'

No answer. She lay looking up at the ceiling, listening. She had often listened like this before going to sleep as a child, wondering if someone would come up and visit her. The ceiling blurred; suggestions of warmth and other modes of being moved in; she slept.

Felix Macguire sat at the console, resting his elbow on the desk and rubbing his chin, as he peered at the big screen. It showed part of a scene at the Herculanean Gate of Pompeii in A.D. 79, with the inhabitants about to be destroyed; a soldier in close-up stood at his post, eyes raised fearfully towards the unknown.

The light values on the soldier's face changed almost unnoticeably as Felix ran back the tape and played over again the words his daughter had spoken.

'. . . had a useful insight into what you meant by reality. A view over the screen is different in some undefined way to a view direct, isn't it?'

He ran it back again listening mainly to the tone of her voice.

'I didn't mean to miss your demonstration, whatever it was, if that is why you are punishing me. If possible I'd like to understand and help. It could be that when watching the big screen I had a useful insight into—'

He clicked her off. Always that pleading and cajoling note in her voice which he recalled from her childhood. A jarring note. No wonder no man had ever married her.

Silence in her room. But it was not the usual silence he received from Number Two bedroom. The usual silence had a sort of thin and rather angular dazed quality unique to itself, resembling the surface of a Vermeer canvas, and with a similar sense almost of *planning* behind it: he thought of it as an intellectual silence and, of course, it differed from the silences in the other rooms. With Anna's occupancy, the silence took on an entirely different weight, a bunched and heavy mottled feeling which he disliked.

The sound levels were so good that he could detect when she was drifting towards sleep. It was her way of eluding reality; a little editing of tape would soon bring her back to her uncomfortable senses.

She roused, sat up suddenly, aware that her mouth had fallen open. Someone was whispering in the room. She had caught the sound of her own voice.

'. . . a useful insight . . .'

Then her father's voice, indistinct, and then her own, perfectly clear:

'Can you hear me, Father?' And his reply:

'Why didn't you watch what your mother and I were doing? You're old enough to learn the facts of life.'

'I didn't mean to miss your demonstration, whatever it was, if that is why you're punishing me.'

'What do you mean, "whatever it was", Anna? Come back into the bedroom and watch – we're just going to start again.'

'If possible, I'd like to understand and help.'

'That's better. Jump in with your mother. You'll soon learn.'

She sat on the edge of the bed, flushing with shame.

'You're right round the bloody twist, Father!' she said aloud. 'For Christ's sake let me out of here and let me go home. I'll never bother you again – you can be sure of that!'

He came in the bedroom door, grinning in an uneasy way.

'Forget all that – just a bit of innocent fun! You see what can be done with reality! Now look, Anna, you present me with a bit of a problem. I'll have to keep you here overnight, so you'd better resign yourself to the fact. Basil Nicholson is coming tomorrow – his visit is very important to me, because for the first time I'm going to present my findings to an impartial outside observer. Nicholson and I have been in communication for months, and he's sufficiently impressed by what I've told him to come and look for himself. You could be useful in more than one way. So you'll have to stay here and behave. If all goes well, you can go home tomorrow afternoon. Okay?'

She just sat and stared at him. The whole business was too horrifying to be believed.

Felix picked up the framed engraving and hung it back on the wall. As he went towards the door, he picked up the saw. He smiled and waved it at her, a gesture part friendly, part menacing.

'Why don't you kill me, Father? You know I can never

140

forgive you – pointing a gun at your own daughter. I saw murder in your eyes, I did.'

He paused with a hand on the door. 'Never forgive? You can't say that. Never forgive? Never? Think what a long journey it is between birth and death. Anything is possible on the way.'

'Go to hell!'

'Think what a long journey you and I have come, Anna! Here we are together in this house; perhaps in one sense we have always been here. Perhaps it doesn't matter that we don't understand each other. Perhaps we hate each other, who knows? We make the journey together. It's like crossing a glacier – in moments of danger, all the various differences between us become unimportant and we are forced to help each other to survive. There's no way of making sense out of such testing journeys until we have the tools to understand what human life is about.'

Anna fumbled in her pocket for a tissue. One nostril was blocked with incipient cold. 'I don't want your philosophizing.'

'But you must understand what I'm saying. Nobody lives out their life without being brought up against a sudden moment when they see themselves as in a screen or mirror and ask themselves, "What am I doing here?" Once, it used to be a religious question. Then people started to interpret it more in socio-economic terms. Your generation tried to answer it in terms of individual escape, and a poor job they made of it. I'm trying to provide an evolutionary solution which will take care of all the other aspects.'

He sounded so reasonable. She was baffled by his changes of mood, always had been.

'If you didn't want to have me here, you should have phoned and told me so. How can you ill-treat me so? I've never harmed you. Pointing that gun at me! I just want to go away – I don't know whether I can ever recover from what you've done to me.'

141

'You keep saying that. Try and pull yourself together, Anna. We're father and daughter – nothing can ever come between us, not even if I had to kill you.'

He had put his arm round her, but now she drew away, looking at him with a face of dread seeing only a blackness in his eyes and a cruel estrangement round his mouth.

'I want to go now, Father, if you don't mind. Back home. Please let me go. I've never done you any harm. Let me go and I'll never bother you again!'

He was as unmoving as stone.

'Never done me any harm? What child has not harmed its parents? Didn't you, every day of your life, come between your mother and me with your insatiable craving for attention? Didn't you drive her into an early grave with your perpetual demands? But for you, wouldn't she be here, on this very bed, with us now?'

'Your evolutionary theory, Father – are you sure you ought to talk about it with Nicholson? Shouldn't you publish a paper on the idea first? Or write to *Nature*, or something?'

He was standing now and looking down on her. She had hunched herself up on the bed with her legs tucked under her.

'You're frightened, aren't you? Why should you be interested in my theories? As—'

The roar of a plane swamped his sentence. For a moment, the room was darkened as the machine passed low overhead. It seemed to distract Macguire's attention. He wandered over to the window.

'The sooner we get control of reality, the better. One of these days, they're not just going to fly over – they'll drop an H-bomb on me, right smack down the chimney, since they can see their warnings don't scare me off.' He turned back to her. 'I must prepare my notes for Nicholson's arrival tomorrow. You'd better come down and clear the

142

place up. If there's time, I'll give you the demonstration I plan to give him and see how you like it. This time, you'd better attend.'

'Oh, I will, I will, Father.'

He walked out of the room, still clutching the saw in his hand. She hesitated, then climbed off the bed and followed him downstairs.

'The front door's locked, by the way, Anna, and I have the key in my pocket.'

'I wasn't thinking of going out.'

'No? Well, it's raining, but just in case you were.'

He went into the living-room, pushed past the partition, and sat down at his console as if nothing had happened. She went into the kitchen, leaned her elbows on the window sill and buried her face in her hands.

After a while, the involuntary shaking in her limbs died away and she looked up. The house was absolutely silent. No, not absolutely. The camera made a faint registration of its presence. With very intent listening, she could hear slight movements from her father in the next room. She looked at her watch, decided to make a cup of tea, and started the soothingly traditional preliminaries of filling the kettle, switching it on, and getting down teapot and tea-caddy from the shelf.

'Like a dutiful daughter, you are making me a cup too.' A loudspeaker.

'Of course, Father.'

How could she persuade him that she loved him? It was impossible, because she did not love him. She had failed to love him. Shouldn't love have sprung up in her spontaneously, however he behaved, the way spring flowers – the modest and incorrigible snowdrops – bud and blossom even in the teeth of chilly winds? The truth was that she understood so little about herself; perhaps she even hoped that he would carry out his direct threats.

When the tea was made, she put everything on a tray and

carried it through to him. Felix smiled and motioned her to put it on a side table.

As she did as he indicated, she saw the carbine. Her father had stood it in the corner behind him. It was ready for action, she thought – was he secretly planning to grab it up and shoot her?

'There are some chocolate biscuits in the cupboard over the sink, if you'd like to get them. You always enjoyed chocolate biscuits, Anna.'

'I still do, as it happens.' She fetched the biscuits.

He drank his tea absently, staring into the miniature screens, switching the view from one or another on to the larger screen, scrutinizing his static universe. Finally he settled on a panorama of the dining-room through Camera Six, with the table, loaded with electronic gear, to one side of the screen and most of it filled by wall and desolate fireplace. This cheerless scene held his attention for so long that his tea grew cold by his elbow.

Anna sat staring towards the carbine.

At last, he sighed and looked up at her.

'Beautiful, isn't it? Human environment with humans abstracted. Almost a new art form – and utterly neglected. But that's neither here nor there.'

Silence.

'Father, would it annoy you to explain to me what you see in the screen?'

'I see everything. The history of the world in that one shot. The grate, designed to burn fossil trees trapped in the earth since they grew in the jungles of the Carboniferous Age. Look at its Art Nouveau motif on the black lead canopy. All obsolete. A great age of mankind gone for ever. Fires will never burn there again, prehistoric energy never be released there. Now the only function of that fireplace is to form part of this picture. The function of the picture is to activate part of my brain. My brain has been activated by retinal designs, formed in this house, never

144

viewed before. I view them every day. They have made me conscious of my own brain structure, which in turn has modified that structure, so that I have been able to fit together facts – facts available to anyone through evolutionary study – and make them into a new whole. A new whole, Anna. You'd never understand.'

He paused and drank down his cold tea.

Keeping herself under control, Anna reflected on the virtue of sanity; it was not half as boring as madness. With sudden impatience, she said, 'Spare me the reasoning, please. Give me the facts. What exactly *is* this theory you keep bragging about?'

He looked rather guiltily up at her. 'You must let it all soak in gradually. It needs practice to understand.'

'I'm sorry, Father, I have a job to go back to. You may not think it important but it is important to me. If you will not show me straightforwardly, then I shall have to leave before it gets dark.'

He digested that. 'I hoped you'd stay and have a bite of supper with me.' His mild manner suggested he had forgotten his earlier threats.

'Why should I, after the way you have treated me? Explain at once or I shall go.'

He shrugged. 'As you will. If you feel up to it.'

Pushing his teacup out of the way, he fiddled with various switches, rose, and messed about behind the partition, before saying, 'Right, then, watch this carefully.'

She dragged her eyes from the weapon in the corner.

The big screen lit. Anna looked with interest, but there was nothing except yet another view of the interior of the house. This was Camera Three working, moving slowly, so that the viewpoint descended from the upper landing to the hall, to a slow moving shot of the hall cupboard and the ever open door through to the garage. In the small section of the garage revealed, the door into the workshop could be seen. Only the eternal gleaming black cables, running across the floor, gave any sense of life. Then she saw a shadow move in the workshop. A man came through into the garage. She gasped.

'It's all right. This is tapex you're watching.'

The man emerged into the hall. It was Felix, rather blank faced, hair slanting across forehead. Without pausing, he moved forward and along the corridor towards the kitchen.

Now the scene was a blank again, unpopulated. The camera eye travelled over it in a leisurely and dispirited fashion. A shadow moved in the depths of the picture and a man passed from workshop to garage. Anna instinctively leaned forward, expecting something – she did not know what: something to frighten her. The man came out of the garage into the hall. It was her father, somewhat blank faced. Without pausing, he moved out of camera range in the direction of the kitchen.

'Keep watching,' Felix ordered.

The screen still showed only the view of the hall, its shadows, and the angles and perspectives created by the doorways beyond – a pattern that, by constant wearying repetition, seemed at once to annihilate sense and to acquire an ominous significance of its own; just as the single note of a dripping tap, listened to long enough, becomes an elusive tune. When something stirred in the shadows beyond the furthest doorway, she was prepared for it, prepared for the man who stepped from the workshop to garage and then, after a pause, from garage to hall. It was her father, wearing his old sweater. Without pausing, blank-faced, he walked towards the kitchen and was lost from view.

The hall was empty. In a brief while, the whole insignificant action was repeated as before. Then it was repeated again. And again. Each time, the same thing happened.

At last the screen went blank, just when Anna thought she would have to scream if it happened once more.

'What have you seen, Anna?'

146

'Oh – you know. You coming out of the garage a million times!'

'Live or on tape?'

'On tape, obviously. The first time round, I thought it was live – well, except that you were here beside me. What does all that prove?'

'If I'd been hidden in the kitchen, you couldn't have told what you saw from live. Or any of the re-runs, if they had been shown first.'

'I suppose not.'

'How many times did you see me come into the hall?'

'I've lost count. Twelve? Eighteen?'

'Nine times. Do you imagine they were all re-runs of one occasion on which I came into the hall?'

'Obviously.'

'It's not obvious. You're wrong. What you witnessed was me coming into the hall on three different occasions – three different days, in fact. Each was re-run three times. And you didn't spot the difference?'

'One time must have been very like another.' She was weary of the nonsense of his solemnity. 'You always looked just the same. The light always looked just the same. Obviously the house always looked just the same.'

'Okay. You're talking about the scientific theory of convergence.'

He pressed a key, ran the videotape until he was once more stepping from garage to hall; then he froze the action. Staring out at his image, he said, 'Obviously, ways of getting from one room to another are always closely alike. Right? So close you mistook them for identical. But they aren't identical. I've tried to remove the difference between one day and the next in this environment, as nearly as I can. Yet I – the living! – am aware of the change between one day and the next, as you were not when witnessing that change on the screen.

'Animals that adapt to similar environments and pursue

the same inclination also tend to resemble each other. However alien the animals themselves may be from each other, there are only a limited number of ways of getting through a doorway or living in a desert or swimming in a sea. To fly, you have to have wings; there are animals which mimic birds in that respect, and they are examples of convergence.'

He pressed a key in front of him, and a shot of the wall of the workshop came up, a grey view with nothing on which to fix attention except three blown-up photographs ranged one under the other on the wall. The photographs depicted three gigantic sea-going creatures, each remarkably similar to the next in its functional streamlined form. Felix left them in view for a while before speaking.

'This is part of the big game I have been hunting for four years, you might say. You know what these creatures are?'

'Are they all sharks?' Anna asked.

A plane roared overhead. The house vibrated, the picture on the screen shimmered and split into a maze of lines and dots. When it reassembled and the noise died, Felix said, 'The top one is a shark. The next one down is a porpoise. The bottom one is an ichthyosaur. They all look alike – prime examples of convergence; yet one is a cartilaginous fish, one a marine mammal, and the other an extinct marine reptile – inwardly, they are nothing alike.'

She fidgeted a little. It was growing dark and she wanted to be away from the house and its insane pedant. The rain had ceased; all was still outside, with the stillness of dripping trees.

'That's hardly a discovery, Father. It has been known for a long time.'

His head drooped, his shoulders slumped. She feared that he was about to burst into one of his insane rages. When he looked up again, his face was distorted with anger, so that she hardly recognized him, as if he had undergone some uncharted Jekyll–Hyde transformation. Instinctively, she took a step back. But he spoke with a measure of calm.

'You do not believe in me, you stupid vegetable . . . Have the wit at least to hear me out when I try to explain everything in layman's language and by analogy. My discovery is that there are creatures as strange as fish and extinct reptiles that go about the world under the same forms as man!'

Anna's first terrified thought was that he was living proof of his own hypothesis. Was there not, in that mottled jowl, that prognathous face, those blazing eyes, something that argued against idiothermous origin and whispered of a reptile brain lurking like an egg inside that bony nest of skull?

He stood up and stood glaring into her face, so that they confronted each other only a few inches apart.

'Reptiles structurally similar to man,' he said. 'Forms almost identical, intentions entirely different. Why is our world being destroyed? Why are the seas being polluted, why are nuclear weapons proliferating towards a holocaust, why do human beings feel increasingly powerless? Because there is an enemy in our midst as different from us as moon is from sun – an enemy intent on wiping out human civilization and reverting to a Jurassic world it still carries in its mind. These enemies are old, Anna, far older than mankind, still carrying a heritage from the Mesozoic in which they were formed, still hoping to bring the Mesozoic back down about our ears!'

With a mingling rush of light and dark in the room, another plane roared overhead, making everything in the room shake, Anna included.

Felix rolled his eyes up to the ceiling. 'There they go! They are gradually assuming power, and power for destruction. Men develop the technology, reptile-men take over its results and use them for destructive ends!'

She clutched at her throat to help bring out her voice. 'Father – it's a terrifying idea you have . . . but . . . but it's – isn't it just your fancy?'

The clouded swollen look was still on his face.

'There is archaeological evidence. Nicholson knows. He has some of it. Evidence from the past is all too scarce. That's my quarrel with Darwinism – a fine picture of evolution has been built up on too little evidence. The layman believes that deceptively whole picture of dinosaurs dying out and mammals developing, and finally homo sapiens rising out of several extinct man forms; but the layman fails to realize how the picture is in fact conjured up merely from a few shards of bone, a broken femur here, a scatter of yellowed teeth there . . . And the picture we now accept is wrong in several vital instances.

'You may know that there is no understanding of why all the species of the two dinosaur genera, the *saurischia* and the *ornithischia*, suddenly died out. Ha! The reason for that lack of understanding is that they did not die out. Both the saurischians and the ornithischians were capable of tremendous variety, adapting to all kinds of conditions, even achieving flight, covering the globe. Both produced creatures which walked on their hind legs like man. But the saurischians also produced a man-creature, evolving from the theropod line.'

'Is there physical proof of the development of this creature?'

'There is no physical proof of the development of any dinosaur – for all we know to the contrary, the brontosaur and tyrannosaur may have popped *out* of existence overnight . . . But a few remains of a late development of reptile-man have been found. You have heard of Neanderthal Man, I presume?'

'Certainly. You aren't going to tell me that Neanderthal Man was a development from a dinosaur!'

'He evolved from the same original stock as the dinosaurs. He was probably always few in number, but he helped kill off the big dinosaurs. The popular folk idea that men were about when the dinosaurs lived is nothing less than the truth – perhaps it's a sort of folk memory.'

'Can I put the light on? It's getting dark in here. But you say the line died out?'

'I didn't say that. The so-called Neanderthal is popularly said to have died out. There's no evidence, though. The Neanderthal reptile-man merged with humanity – mammal-humanity, and we have never been able to sort them out since.'

She stood by the door, hand on the light switch, again thinking of flight. When the overhead light came on, it made the images of the three marine creatures on the screen appear faint and spectral, more suited to move through air than water.

'Father, my headache has come back. May I go upstairs and lie down in my room to think about what you have told me?'

He moved a little nearer to her.

'Do you believe what I have told you? Do you understand? Are you capable of understanding?'

'How is it that modern medicine has not tracked down these reptile-men if they still exist, by blood-analysis or something?'

'It has. But it has misinterpreted the evidence. I won't go into the whole complex question of blood-grouping. Another problem is that reptile-men and human stock now interbreed. The lines are confused. There is reason to think that venereal disease is the product of interbreeding – another intravenous way in which the two species seek to destroy each other. Do you want some aspirins?'

'I have some eau-de-cologne in my case in the car. May I go and get it?'

'You go upstairs. I'll get your case for you.'

Hesitating, she looked at him. Not liking what she saw, she moved reluctantly and walked along the hall corridor, turned right, and went up the stairs under the eye of Camera Three, holding to the banisters as she went. She paused again on the landing. Reptile-men! Then she went ahead into the bedroom, glanced hopelessly up at 'Faithful Unto Death', sullen in the twilight, and lay down. She could have locked herself in but what was the point? In his madness, her father would break the door down whenever he felt like it. Perhaps he would come up and kill her; perhaps he imagined she was of reptilian stock.

She played with that idea, imagining the strange and aberrant allegiances it might give her with gloomy green unflowering plants, with damp stones, with immense shapes that moved only when prompted by the sun, and with languid spans of time which could find no true lodgement within the consciousness of man. The idea of being cold-blooded alone made her tremble where she lay, and clutch at the blankets for warmth.

There was a dull light in the room, gloomy, green, and unflowering. Another plane blundered over, shaking the house.

Downstairs, he heard and felt the plane go over. He raised his heavy eyes up towards its path, imagining it furry and coleopterous while the room vibrated, saying to it, 'One day, you too will lie broken and stony in a shattered layer of sandstone.'

He stood before the big screen, Camera One trained on him, throwing his image over his body. Eyes, mouth, head, limbs, vibrated, became double and detached, then settled back as the noise died.

A memory came back to him from far away that he had said he would go and get Anna's case from her car.

Moving with lethargy, he crossed to the console and set Camera One moving until it was trained through the living-room door to the dining-room door. This was the nearest he could get to covering the back door; some day, he must install a tenth camera in the passage, so that the back door was surveyed. All he could see on the screen now was the ugly concatenation of angles formed by the two doors be-

tween them. He walked out into the passage and headed
down it, to the door with two glass panels in its frame which
he always kept locked. He unlocked it, opened it, went out.

To his right stretched the length of the back of the house.
At right angles to it, another wall stood along the left,
punctuated by scullery and pantry windows. An uneven path
flanked his walk. He moved slowly along it. There had
been flagstones of good York stone underfoot, but weeds
and grass had covered them. Blank eyes of scullery and
pantry surveyed him.

The light was leaden now. Time and twilight were con-
gealed and fixed like a murdered eye. Like something viewed in a long mirror, he was embedded far in the past, together with gymnosperms, woodlice, the first ungainly
amphibians and things still unidentified by the peeping gaze
of man.

When he turned left round by the corner of the wood-
shed, Macguire was only a few feet away from the sterile
green wire fence. He knew a lot of things about the colour
green; it, more than any colour, was involved in the guilty
story of downfall.

He turned left again, pushing aside overgrown branches
of elder. They still flowered, individual florets looming up
before his eyes like galaxies in some dim-lit and cluttered
universe. Now he was stalking along the south-west side of
the house. The weeds of high summer crushed and sprang
under his footfall.

There was her car, low under the overhanging branches
of trees. Every year, the beeches grew nearer and nearer to
the house. Some of them already nuzzled their first tender
branches against the brick.

He stood glaring through the windows at the seats within,
awaiting people. It was shabby and vacant in there, another
unwelcoming human environment, depopulated. On the
back seat lay a small case. Macguire pulled open the rear
door, grasped the handle of the case, and dragged it out. He

stood with it where he was, his other hand touching the car, staring at his daughter. Anna had come round the front of the house; she held his carbine in an efficient way, and was pointing it at his stomach. He looked at her face and saw it too belonged with the lost gymnosperms, woodlice, and amphibians hidden long ago behind the pantry, engendering only extinction.

'You can go if you don't shoot me, Anna. I'm the only one with the theory complete, although there are people everywhere piecing it together. It's a matter of time . . . It's not a race. I mean, there's no excitement – it's too late now for man to beat the reptile-men; they've had too long and they are virtually in control. Look at the light under these trees – if you understand such things, the light alone will tell you we're defeated. So there's no point in shooting.'

'I'm going to shoot.' The words came from her mouth. He watched the diagram of it, thinking how easy it was to understand human speech once you had the basic knowledge of the working anatomy of jaw and thorax and the formation of phonemes in the larynx by careful control of air, and how those sounds were carried into the listening labyrinths of those present. His daughter had the science of the whole thing off perfectly.

'I could show you yards of tapex – proof. Proof of all I say. I'm the only one who has studied a human being long enough. I've seen myself, caught myself off guard, I have to regard myself as heteromorphic. The reptile moves in my veins, too.'

'Move away from the car.'

He said, feeling the stiff discomfort of fear contort his lips and teeth and tongue, 'Anna, this isn't the time of day . . . Just when I'm getting control of reality . . . Look, you're alien too. It's strong in you. Believe me. That's why you're so hostile. You're more lizard than I. Let me go! I won't hurt you! Let me show you!'

The gun-point lowered slightly. A moth blundered through the space between their two ghastly faces and fell under the trees.

'What do you mean?'

'I got it on tapex. You can come in and see for yourself. Camera Number Eight. It's betrayed in certain movements. Unhuman movements. The gesture of the hand, the way a knee hinges, spinal tension, hip flexibility, a dozen details of facial expression. Oh, I've observed them all in myself. One hundred and thirty-one differences docketed. Throughout life, human beings are motivated to watch others and not themselves, right from early years when they begin to learn by imitation. I realized years ago I was not fully human. With age, you become less human, the antique lizard shows through more and more – after all, it's the basic stock. That's why old people turn against human pleasures. Now, in your case, you've never had much time for human pleasures—'

'Father—'

Afterwards, she wondered if he had begun to fall before she fired. The first shot curved the top half of his body forward. She fired again. This time he jerked backwards, still standing, so that she saw how long and dark and lined his throat was. His mouth opened a little. She had thought that he was looking down his nose and laughing at her, totally unharmed. She fired a third bullet, but was already trembling so violently that it missed.

An airbus came sizzling over the property so low that she fired again in sheer panic. The bullet whistled into the leaves of the trees, and still her father stood there, rocking a little, hands like claws digging into his belly. Then he fell over backwards, legs straight. When he hit the ground, the force of the fall caused his arms to spring out sideways. He lay there among the mid-summer weeds in that attitude of unknowing, and never moved again. The beeches dripped on him, the erosions of his last July.

155

His hair was quite wet before Anna managed to move again.

She dropped the gun, then had the presence of mind to fumble it up again and toss it into the car. She picked up the little case and tossed that into the car. She stood over the body.

'Father?' she asked it.

It continued to make its gesture of unknowing.

Fighting her palsy, she climbed into the driving seat of the car. After several attempts, she got the motor going and managed to back away to the front of the house. She gave a last look into that deep grey-green past under the beeches where time had ceased, and drove towards the front gates.

As she passed through them, bumping on to the cul-de-sac road, she experienced a flash of memory. She thought of the electricity still burning, the camera still processing the spirit of the empty house, the big screen still registering daylight dying between an ugly angle of doors, the inhuman sequence of mounting time slithering into tapex.

But she did not pause, certainly did not turn back. Instead, she pressed her foot more firmly to the accelerator, flicked on the side-lights, hunched herself over the wheel to control her shaking, forged ahead towards the angle of tiny roads between her and Ashmansford.

She stared ahead. The shaggy beeches outside the car, blue with advancing night, were reflected momentarily in her eyeballs. Overhead, another plane roared, its landing lights blazing, coming into roost.

The world's greatest science fiction authors now available in Panther Books

Robert Silverberg

Earth's Other Shadow	£1.50	☐
The World Inside	£1.50	☐
Tower of Glass	£1.50	☐
Recalled to Life	£1.50	☐
Invaders from Earth	£1.50	☐
Master of Life and Death	£1.50	☐

J G Ballard

The Crystal World	£2.50	☐
The Drought	£2.50	☐
Hello America	£1.50	☐
The Disaster Area	£2.50	☐
Crash	£2.50	☐
Low-Flying Aircraft	£2.50	☐
The Atrocity Exhibition	£1.50	☐
The Venus Hunters	£2.50	☐
The Day of Forever	£2.50	☐
The Unlimited Dream Company	£2.50	☐
Concrete Island	£2.50	☐

Philip Mann

The Eye of the Queen	£1.95	☐

To order direct from the publisher just tick the titles you want and fill in the order form.

The world's greatest science fiction authors now available in Panther Books

Bob Shaw
The Ceres Solution	£1.50	☐
A Better Mantrap	£1.50	☐
Orbitsville	£1.95	☐
Orbitsville Departure	£1.95	☐

William Burroughs
Nova Express	£1.25	☐

Arthur C Clarke
2010: Odyssey Two	£1.95	☐

Harry Harrison
Rebel in Time	£1.95	☐

The To The Stars Trilogy
Homeworld	£1.95	☐
Wheelworld	£1.95	☐
Starworld	£1.95	☐

James Kahn
World Enough, and Time	£1.95	☐
Time's Dark Laughter	£1.95	☐

Christopher Stasheff
A Wizard in Bedlam	£1.25	☐
The Warlock in Spite of Himself	£1.25	☐
King Kobold	£1.50	☐
The Warlock Unlocked	£1.95	☐

Doris Lessing
'Canopus in Argos: Archives'
Shikasta	£2.50	☐
The Marriage Between Zones Three, Four, and Five	£1.95	☐
The Sirian Experiments	£1.95	☐
The Making of the Representative for Planet 8	£1.95	☐

David Mace
Demon 4	£1.50	☐
Nightrider	£1.95	☐

To order direct from the publisher just tick the titles you want and fill in the order form.

All these books are available at your local bookshop or newsagent, or can be ordered direct from the publisher.,

To order direct from the publisher just tick the titles you want and fill in the form below.

Name_____

Address _____

_____

Send to:
Panther Cash Sales
PO Box 11, Falmouth, Cornwall TR10 9EN.

Please enclose remittance to the value of the cover price plus:

UK 45p for the first book, 20p for the second book plus 14p per copy for each additional book ordered to a maximum charge of £1.63.

BFPO and Eire 45p for the first book, 20p for the second book plus 14p per copy for the next 7 books, thereafter 8p per book.

Overseas 75p for the first book and 21p for each additional book.

Panther Books reserve the right to show new retail prices on covers, which may differ from those previously advertised in the text or elsewhere.